MW00946613

Taming the Beastly Duke of Ashbourne

A Clean Regency Romance Novel

Martha Barwood

Table of Contents

Prologue

"William?"

Nathanial looked around at the garden, taking in the sunlight, the way it dappled across the leaves and the colors in the flowers. Everything seemed a little too bright, a little too beautiful but all the same, Nathanial smiled.

"Ashbourne!"

He turned, seeing William running across the garden toward him. Reaching out both hands, Nathanial caught up his younger brother, whirling him around as his younger brother laughed... only for the light in the garden to begin to fade. Holding his brother tight, Nathanial looked around, his eyes flaring in fright as light began to disappear, replaced by shadow and darkness.

What was happening?

"William?"

His brother was no longer in his arms. Caught by fear, Nathanial let out a cry of fright – and suddenly he was sitting up in bed, cold sweat breaking out across his forehead, his breathing ragged.

"William." Closing his eyes, Nathanial let out a slow breath, trying to stop his heart from hammering so furiously. The nightmare had repeated itself yet again and, even though William was safe, the darkness now a distant memory, he simply could not remove it from his mind.

"I failed him." Muttering to himself, Nathanial pushed one hand through his dark hair, wiping the sweat from his forehead. No matter how many days passed, that memory continued to linger in his mind. The way he had failed William, the way he had almost brought about the death of his younger brother by his negligence would not leave him. It was what drove him to consider his character with almost every waking moment, what brought about his nightmares and the fear which wrapped a coldness around his heart. A calm night's sleep seemed to evade him no matter what tinctures his doctor suggested.

Nathanial feared that this nightmare would never leave him.

Chapter One

"Did you enjoy your breakfast, Lady Amelia?"

Amelia smiled as her maid bobbed a curtsy. "I did, thank you, Abby."

"Might I be of any assistance to you? What are your intentions this morning?"

Amelia gestured to the writing desk. "Why, we are writing our invitations for our literary salon this morning!"

"Ah yes, I do remember. Might I bring you a tray of tea and biscuits?"

"Yes, that would be lovely." Still smiling, Amelia put out both hands either side. "And if you should see Charlotte, then please do ask her to join me! She is meant to be deciding with me who it is we should be inviting."

With a nod and a smile, the maid stepped out and left Amelia alone. Walking to the writing desk, Amelia sat down and picked up the list that Charlotte and she had made only yesterday, though it was not yet complete. Sunshine shone through the windows and she lifted her gaze to the window, rising to her feet to walk across the room and looking back out to the gardens of her father's manor house.

It was a beautiful place, especially in the summer time and Amelia found herself smiling gently as she took in a long breath and let it out again, contentedly. This was where she felt herself happy, felt herself joyous and contented and even though her father was threatening to take her sister and her to London for the upcoming Season, Amelia was not certain that he would do so. She knew just how much he loved the Stanton estate, remembering with a smile how, last year, both her mother and he would often walk through the rose garden together. Yes, they had gone to London for Charlotte's come out but they had not lingered, seeming eager to return to their estate. Of course, it was time for her to make her come out but another year at home would not make any great difference, would it?

"I am sorry I am so tardy!"

Turning, Amelia laughed as Charlotte flew into the room, her cheeks a little pink. "Pray, do not worry."

"I was out in the gardens," Charlotte told her, flopping into a chair. "It is such a fine morning that I did not want to be indoors. But then I quite forgot that we were to be writing out our invitations and when your maid found me, I came back here as quickly as I could."

"I know that you do not particularly like writing invitations but it must be done if we are to have a successful literary event," Amelia reminded her, waving the list in front of her face. "I do enjoy walking through the roses, however so mayhap we might do so together this afternoon?"

Charlotte smiled. "Yes, of course. I would like that."

"Good." Amelia gestured to the paper in front of her. "So, are we certain that all those we have thought of are those that we wish to invite?"

"Yes, I think so." Taking the list from Amelia, Charlotte read through it quickly and then nodded. "This is to be a great event, I am sure. You, especially, will find it a most enjoyable event, will you not? You do love company and the like and you have read a few books upon occasion. I am sure it will be an excellent event."

Smiling to herself, Amelia walked to the writing desk and sat back down. "Yes, I dare say I will enjoy this event, though I am a little anxious to know who will be attending!"

"Though not everyone who comes will find it to be so exhilarating, I am sure." Charlotte offered her a wry smile. "Some will come merely for the entertainment – or for the games of cards that Father is sure to have put out for some of the gentlemen."

"Mayhap that is true but I am certain we will have a good many discussions, though there will also be some readings."

"Readings?"

"Yes, of course. We cannot have a literary event without some people reading from their favourite passages or the like." Amelia lifted an eyebrow. "Have you prepared something?"

Charlotte's eyes widened in surprise. "No, I have not."

"Well, you still have time," Amelia replied, picking out her first piece of paper, ready to write the first invitation. "Both of us ought to read aloud since we are organizing and hosting the event and, since it is still some days away, we do have a good deal of time to prepare. Even a poem or two would suffice, Charlotte, I am sure." Seeing the slight grey to her sister's pallor, Amelia hid a smile. Charlotte clearly did not want to read but Amelia was sure it would be required. "Now, I did have one question for you." Lifting her gaze, she looked directly at her sister. "Ought we to invite the Beastly Duke?"

Her sister's shoulders slumped. "*Why* should we invite him?"

"Because his estate is near to our father's," Amelia replied, lifting one shoulder and letting it fall. "It is not as though we expect him to attend, is it? He is a gentleman who likes to keep company with only himself and therefore, he will not be inclined to accept."

"Then why should we bother to invite him?" Charlotte propped one elbow on the chair arm and then dropped her head to her hand. "There is no reason to send out an invitation or, indeed, to waste our time even writing it to him!"

"But we might be seen as rude if we do not." Amelia sighed and looked down the list of those she wished to invite. "It will not take me but a few minutes to write to him and, as I have said, he will, no doubt, refuse to attend."

Charlotte rolled her eyes. "He is a gentleman I do not understand. Why does he spend his days in his own company when he has so many fine gentlemen and ladies about him? He has his mother residing in the house with him, I have heard, though I have also heard whispers that she cannot linger in his company for any length of time and is often away from home!"

"I do not know if that is true nor why he wishes for his own company," Amelia replied, quietly, looking back at her sister. "I have heard that there was something that occurred with his younger brother some time ago and thereafter, though it took some time for his younger brother to recover, all was well. The Duke himself, however, has lingered in darkness and does not like to be in the company of anyone. It is as though he lingers in that dreadful moment and does not allow it to pass." Her heart softened with a sudden sympathy though she quickly shook her head. "I do not understand him, however. He is a gentleman who seems to dislike the company of others. Which is why, Charlotte, I do not think that he will come to our literary event."

Charlotte let out a slow breath and closed her eyes. "Very well. If you think that it would be best to invite him – even though he will not attend – then let us do so."

Amelia smiled at her sister's obvious reluctance. "I think that it is the best idea, my dear sister. After all, we want to make certain that we are doing all that we ought to be doing and do not bring any question of propriety to our father. He will, no doubt, have very little interest in our company and certainly will not enjoy the literary readings but all the same, we want to make certain no-one questions why this person or that person was not invited."

With a nod, Charlotte made to rouse herself from her chair only for the door to open and Abby the maid to come back into the room, a tray in her hands.

"Here we are," she said, that warm tone speaking of the many years that she had served Amelia and Charlotte, though she was now Amelia's lady's maid. "Do you wish for me to serve two cups of tea for you both?"

"Yes, please." Amelia shot a quick, winking glance to her sister. "We will need all the sustenance we can get if we are to write each of these invitations by luncheon!"

Charlotte let out a groan but did get to her feet, ready now to help Amelia. Laughing, Amelia handed her sister a piece of paper, moved a little further down the writing table and set to work – and the very first invitation she wrote was to the Beastly Duke himself.

"You invited the Beastly Duke?"

Amelia nodded, a little surprised at her mother's astonishment. "Yes, Mama, I did. The invitations have not gone out as yet, however. They will be sent away tomorrow."

"I do hope you are not expecting him to accept?" Lady Stanton asked, as Amelia quickly glanced to her sister, who immediately began to shake her head. "The Beastly Duke is not inclined to spend time with anyone – least of all those who wish to discuss such things as books!"

"No, Mama, we are not expecting him to attend. Though I did think that it would be wise to invite him, just so that we did not offend him by our lack of invitation when everyone else in the vicinity received one."

Lord Stanton harrumphed though when Amelia looked to him, he was not only smiling but nodding. "That was very considerate, my dear. Though as your mother has said, do not expect him to attend. That gentleman does not like to set foot out of his estate unless he absolutely has no other choice but to do so!"

"And why is that, Father?" Amelia asked, her interest piqued. "I have only seen the Duke of Ashbourne on one occasion before and he seemed rather ill tempered and disinclined towards company, I must say."

"That is because he is." Lord Stanton lifted both shoulders. "His younger brother almost drowned some years ago now and though I do remember that there were many doctors and physicians sent for, the young lad recovered very well. However, since that time, the Duke of Ashbourne has been entirely disinclined towards company. He has not shown any interest in attending any social events and though he has shown his face at some rare occasions, I do believe it is only because his mother desired to attend." His lips quirked. "I do recall that the last time he came to a ball or some such thing, he simply stood to the back of the room, his arms crossed over his chest and his expression so furious, no-one dared approach him!"

Amelia tilted her head, finding herself a little intrigued. "How very strange. I should like to know what it is that makes him behave so."

"I am sure many a person would, given that he is not only a Duke but also very wealthy indeed. However," Lady Stanton continued, with a wry smile, "he seems determined not to be known and thus, we are left with many more questions than we have answers."

Charlotte and Amelia exchanged a glance and Amelia could immediately guess what it was her sister was thinking. "I think I shall have one more invitation to send, Mama," she murmured, seeing the gleam in Charlotte's eyes. "You say that the Duke of Ashbourne attends occasions only when his mother desires to join? Then mayhap we should also invite Lady Ashbourne also, though I have heard she is not often at home. Mayhap that will be enough to convince the Duke of Ashbourne to show his face."

Lady Stanton laughed, shaking her head lightly. "Are you truly so intrigued by him?"

"I confess that I am."

"As do I," Charlotte added, a little flush in her cheeks. "He is so very mysterious, I think, though that is quite the opposite of what I said to Amelia at the beginning of the day."

Lord Stanton chuckled, shaking his head. "My dear girls, you will soon find that this mysterious gentleman will be nothing more than a disappointment. He will come and he will stand in this room and he will say and do nothing that will bring you any contentment. He will be the very worst of guests and you will wonder why you ever thought to invite him."

Her curiosity not in the least bit dimmed, Amelia smiled back at her father. "That may be so but I am determined to do such a thing regardless. I am sure that another invitation can be written today, ready for them all to be sent out tomorrow morning."

Her father laughed and spread his hands. "Do as you think best, my dear. "

Seeing the smile on Charlotte's face, Amelia considered for a few moments longer and then nodded firmly. "Then I shall write it this very evening – and we shall see whether or not the Beastly Duke can be persuaded to attend our literary event… and what an interesting event it shall be!"

Chapter Two

"Your Grace."

The quiet, stilted tones of his footman made Nathanial scowl. He knew all too well that his staff were not particularly enamored by him as a master. He was much too sour-faced and sharp tongued to make any of his footmen or maids happy.

Not that such a thing mattered to him.

"What is it?"

"You have an invitation, Your Grace."

Still scowling, Nathanial turned his head to look, having been absorbed in his own papers for the last hour since he had broken his fast. He did not like being disturbed. "An invitation?"

"Yes, Your Grace. Your mother has received one also and would urge you to read it just as soon as possible."

Nathanial rolled his eyes and held out his hand for the invitation. He had no intention whatsoever of attending any event, no matter what it was. He was not someone inclined towards company and, given his lack of attendance at such things, he would have thought that the society around him would have known of his inclination by now. Turning the invitation over, he recognized the seal of the Marquess of Stanton and, breaking it, unfolded the invitation and read their supposed eager desire to have him attend their literary event.

A quick glance around his study told Nathanial why they might think of inviting him to such a thing. After all, he was inclined to a great deal of study and reading though it was not the sort of thing that young ladies would enjoy, he supposed – and this invitation *was* from the younger of the Stanton ladies. What had possessed her to think that he would be glad to come to such an occasion, he could not even begin to imagine.

"I shall not be attending. You can tell my mother that – "

"You can tell your mother yourself."

Nathanial shifted in his chair as his mother strode into the room. "Were you eavesdropping, Mother?"

"If you mean that I was standing outside your study and listening to your response to Montrose here, then yes." Gesturing to the butler, she nodded to him. "You are excused, Montrose. Thank you for doing as I asked."

Nathanial tilted his head. "I thought they were *my* staff, Mother."

"They were mine before they were yours," came the sharp response. "Now, Ashbourne, tell me why you will not attend this occasion? It is the perfect opportunity for you to go and discuss your many, *many* opinions on all the books you have been reading and the like."

Nathanial sniffed. "I do not think that the sort of books I read are the sort of books they would like to discuss." He gestured to the invitation. "It says that there are to be literary readings. Do you really think that they would be inclined to listen to a reading from one of my books? Or are they not, as I suspect, much more inclined to seek out readings from romantic poetry and ridiculous novels?"

His mother lifted her chin. "You speak as though those novels and poetry are somehow lesser to what *you* engage your mind with, my son. Do not think of yourself too highly, I beg of you. It is prideful."

"And I will not be guilt ridden into attending," Nathanial replied, with a sharp smile. "If you wish to attend then write and accept. But I shall not be."

"And why not? What is it that ties you here?" His mother's tone softened just a little but Nathanial scowled, his brow furrowing as she came to sit down opposite him. "If it is to do with William — which I suspect your dark moods are always about — then you need to set that path aside."

Nathanial looked away. "Mother, I – "

"Your nightmares have continued, have they not?" Lady Ashbourne tilted her head, in the very same way he himself often did. "I heard the maids whispering."

"They ought not to be. Tell me who you heard it from and I shall have them sent away from this estate at once!"

Lady Ashbourne sighed and sat back in her chair a little more. "It could not be that there is concern for you in that, could there? That they do not speak of you with malice or ill will?"

Snorting, Nathanial rolled his eyes. "Mother, I am very aware of what my staff think of me."

12

"That does not mean that they cannot speak with concern, my son." Lady Ashbourne let out another breath. "It pains me to see you sitting here alone. Why are you doing so? Why can you not leave this study for even a single hour, it seems!"

Nathanial's scowl lingered. "I am quite contented here."

"I do not believe you. You cannot be contented sitting here year after year and only ever emerging when William returns home."

At the name of his younger brother, Nathanial flinched and then despised himself for it. No doubt his mother would have seen it and, in observing it, would know what troubled him despite his protestations that there was nothing that worried him.

"William is a very happy, contented, healthy young man." Lady Ashbourne's voice had gentled all the more. "My dear boy, you need not worry about him."

"He has a limp."

Lady Ashbourne shook her head. "It is a very minor limp, Ashbourne. And he is alive which is the most important thing, is it not?"

Nathanial closed his eyes as memories began to flood him. He had been laughing and playing with his friends in the middle of his father's estate grounds. They had been foolish, choosing to walk across a large branch which they had placed across one of the rivers which ran through the gardens. They had always been warned to be careful around it but he had been of an age where he had given no heed to such things.

William, of course, had been younger and determined to impress Nathanial and his friends though he had done his best to ignore him. Too late had he realized that William had attempted to walk across the branch. Too late had he realized that his brother was not present and too late had he sprinted to the pond and made his way across the branch to pull him to safety. William had been grey, his eyes closed. When Nathanial had passed his brother to his friends, his own clothes pulling down to the pond with the wet, William's foot had caught under the branch. Not only had he been so utterly irresponsible as to miss where his brother had gone, he had then caused him further trauma in his poor handling of William as he had pulled him from the pond.

"Do not think of that."

Nathanial looked sharply at his mother who was smiling gently. Somehow, she had known how his thoughts were being tormented.

"Think on how you revived your brother," she said, softly. "Your father found you carrying him back to the house – conscious."

"And screaming."

"But that is better than being drowned, Nathanial."

It was not often that his mother spoke to him in such a tone but this was one of complete sympathy – a balm that Nathanial refused to settle upon his heart. This was not what he deserved, not what he wanted. All he desired at present was to be by himself, to drown himself in books so that he would not have to think of that painful memory that simply would not leave his mind.

"I will write to Lady Amelia."

Without warning, his mother rose from her chair and walked to the door, perhaps seeing that he desired his own company. "And I will accept on behalf of both of us."

"You will do no such thing!" Nathanial rose from his chair, walking across the room to where his mother stood, though she did not so much as flinch. "I do not want to attend and therefore, I shall remain at home. If you wish to join them then please, take the carriage, take whatever you wish but I shall – "

"You shall attend with me."

The cool, crisp words of his mother made Nathanial's frustrations grow all the more. She was either unwilling to listen to him or determined not to and both were irritating him utterly.

"Mother, please understand. I have no intention of making my way to societal events. I have no desire to be in company with any other. William will soon be home for the Season and – "

"Your brother is to remain in London for the Season."

Nathanial stopped dead, his eyes flaring. "I beg your pardon?"

"I received a letter from him yesterday. He is going to be remaining in London for the Season, though he does intend to return at Christmastime."

His heart ripped from his chest as he took in a long breath. Seeing William, being certain that he was quite well, was a balm and a comfort that he needed year on year. It was his time to see

14

that his brother, albeit with a slight limp, was still hale and hearty, an occasion for them to be in one another's company so they might reminisce and laugh together. It happened every year and thereafter, once William had returned to Eton or now, given that he was finished there, back to his own estate, Nathanial would slowly begin to retreat back into the darkness and the heaviness that came with it. He would remember the limp that his brother had, would fear for his brother that he would never find a suitable bride thanks to his infirmity which was, of course, Nathanial's fault.

"You will see your brother again, of course," his mother continued, as Nathanial tried to breathe in past the tightness in his lungs. "He will come back to the estate for a time but he must spend more time at his own estate – or in London – now. The time for him to step into his role is at hand and, therefore, he considers what he requires for his future." Her eyebrow arched. "Namely, a bride."

Nathanial's mouth fell open. "Mother! One moment you are asking me to go to a literary event and now you are asking me to go and seek out a bride?!"

She smiled. "I am. After all, you are a Duke and you must continue the family line, must you not?"

A heaviness settled on Nathanial's heart and he shook his head. "I would rather go to the literary event rather than have you speak to me about matrimony, Mother."

A quiet laugh escaped her and with a shake of her head, Lady Ashbourne left the room, leaving Nathanial once more to his solitude.

Taking in a long, slow breath, Nathanial closed his eyes and waited for the relief that his solitude would bring him... but it did not come. Instead, he felt his mother's words about continuing the line settling on his heart and weighing it down. That was one of his responsibilities, he knew, but it was not something he was able to consider. Not as yet. That would require him to step out into society, to go to the *ton* and seek out someone to come and share this house – and his life – with him. At the present moment, that was not something he could even consider, not when his life was so very contained within these four walls.

Letting out an exclamation of frustration, Nathanial rose from his chair and strode to his desk. Pulling out a piece of fresh writing paper, he sat and picked up his quill, writing out his reply before his mother could change his mind. Writing his regret – none of which he truly had – he let Lady Amelia know that he would not be attending the literary salon but thanked her for the invitation.

And then he scrawled up the letter and began again. This time, he did not add in a single word of thanks but stated clearly and concisely that he would *not* be in attendance. Silently, he hoped that this would communicate to the young lady that he was not desirous of such invitations so that he would never receive such a thing again.

Rising, he rang the bell and then returned to seal his letter. When the butler arrived, Nathanial handed him the note immediately.

"Have this delivered at once and inform my mother once it is sent."

The butler blinked. "Inform her, Your Grace?"

"Tell her that my response to Lady Amelia has been sent and that I am steadfast in my determination not to attend," Nathanial stated, clearly. "Her own response will come later, I am sure."

Dismissing the butler, he waited until the door closed before letting himself relax just a little. Again, he waited for the relief, for the contentment to come but instead, all he could think of was his mother's remarks about his own unmarried state and his brother William's determination to stay in London.

He was used to being alone. He had told himself he liked it. So why now did he feel so very unsettled?

Chapter Three

Amelia smiled as Charlotte finished her reading, clapping lightly when her sister bobbed a quick curtsy. Charlotte was to be the last to read before they broke for luncheon and rising to her feet, Amelia quickly thanked everyone for their steady interest, their own readings and encouraged them all to make their way to the dining room.

"You did so very well, Charlotte!" Amelia exclaimed, as the other guests began to make their way out of the room. "Thank you for doing that. I know that you were nervous."

"I was." Charlotte let out a slightly shuddering breath. "I am glad it is done."

"I would not have known you were in the least bit agitated."

Both Amelia and Charlotte turned at the voice, a smile quickly spreading across Amelia's face as the lady smiled warmly at Charlotte.

"I thank you, Your Grace," Charlotte replied, greeting the lady warmly. "You are very kind to say so."

"I do hope you will do a reading also, if you wish it?" Amelia suggested, seeing the lady nod. "I think the other guests would be as delighted as I to hear you."

Lady Ashbourne smiled. "You are very kind." Her smile slipped. "I am sorry that my son would not join us today. I think it would have been very good for him to be present but alas, I could not convince him."

"No?"

Lady Ashbourne shook her head. "He is a man who is inclined to linger in his own company, though he has not always done so. He will soon have to find a wife, however, so I have been encouraging him to consider making his way to London."

Amelia blinked, a little surprised that a gentleman should have to be encouraged to go to London. She had thought that it was a delight for each and every gentleman to be present in the London Season.

"My younger son, William – the Marquess of Highcroft – will be present, however." Lady Ashbourne lifted her shoulders lightly. "So I shall be pleased with that." Tilting her head, she looked first

17

at Amelia and then to Charlotte. "You have made your come out, Lady Charlotte, have you not?"

"I have, yes. Last Season."

"And you did not attend, Lady Amelia?"

Amelia shook her head no.

"Then you will, no doubt, go to London *this* Season, yes?"

Wondering why Lady Ashbourne was asking her such a thing, Amelia felt heat rise up in her face though she quickly pushed it away with nothing more than a smile. "My father is threatening to take me to London, yes."

Lady Ashbourne's expression lifted. "You do not wish to go?"

"I – it is not that I do not *wish* to go," Amelia replied, trying to find an explanation for how she felt at present. "It is only that I do so very much enjoy being a part of my father's estate, particularly at this time of year. The flowers are so very beautiful and the grounds take my breath from me whenever I have the chance to walk through them."

A small smile touched the edges of Lady Ashbourne's lips. "I quite understand. Though London has many of its own beauties, also, I must say. It would be a pity for you to miss it all."

"Oh, I am sure that my father will take us both to London either this Season or the next," Charlotte replied, taking Lady Ashbourne's attention from Amelia. "I do not particularly mind, much as my sister does, but that is because – "

"Because you have an engagement already secured, yes, I have heard." Lady Ashbourne tilted her head. "To the Marquess of Stirling, yes?"

Amelia looked to Charlotte, wondering if her sister would be at all upset that Lady Ashbourne had mentioned Charlotte's impending engagement to a gentleman she did not know very well but Charlotte only smiled and confirmed that yes, this was who it was to be. The two ladies continued in conversation on this subject for some time and Amelia merely listened, recalling the moment Charlotte had consented to marry Lord Stirling. The gentleman was the son of the late Marquess who had been dear friends with their own father and thought there had been a hope that the two families might join in marriage in some way. Amelia had been glad that her sister had never been forced into this engagement but had been given her own choice – but evidently, she had been contented with the gentleman himself once they had met and had spoken at length on a few occasions. Amelia did not know Lord Stirling particularly well as yet – neither did her sister – but Lord Stirling was to come to reside with them all very soon, once some business matters were attended to. Given that he lived in Scotland, it was some distance to come and Amelia continued to push the thought of the engagement and marriage from her mind, for the thought of her sister being so very far away was rather heartbreaking.

"Then you will have your choice of gentlemen, should you go to London, Lady Amelia."

Amelia looked back to Lady Ashbourne, fixing a polite smile to her face. "It would seem so, Your Grace, though I am certain there will be a good many ladies there also."

Lady Ashbourne chuckled. "Ah, but there will not be very many daughters of marquesses present, my dear. You are certain to be the object of every gentleman's eye, I am sure of it! You must tell me if you are to go to London. I would be very glad to introduce you to my son."

Amelia blinked. "Which one, might I ask?"

Lady Ashbourne laughed as though Amelia had said something humorous. "My son William, of course. Though I should like you to come and visit me at the estate?"

A thrill ran up Amelia's spine. "That is very kind of you, Your Grace."

"Oh, it would be a pleasure for me! If my son will not come out in company then mayhap I will force company upon him!"

"And this would be your *other* son," Charlotte put in, sounding a little uncertain. "The Duke of Ashbourne?"

"Yes, that is just so." Lady Ashbourne smiled, looking from Charlotte to Amelia and back again. "You would like to come and call, I hope? Your mother would be more than welcome also, though I should say I would like to know you both a little better. I know your mother well!"

"We would be very glad to call upon you, Your Grace," Amelia replied, quickly. "Thank you for such a kind invitation."

A brightness came into Lady Ashbourne's smile. "But of course. What about Friday afternoon? You could come to take tea or, in fact, stay for dinner? It is a long drive and I would be glad to make certain you are well fed before you return home!"

Amelia looked to Charlotte, seeing her sister nodding. "Again, you are very kind, Your Grace. We could come around midday? And then depart once we have sat with you for dinner."

"Excellent!" Turning around, Lady Ashbourne looked all around the room but most of the guests had already quit the room. "I will go in search of your mother and tell her all. Do excuse me."

"But of course." Amelia smiled as she took Charlotte's arm, leading her towards the door so they too might go to the dining room. "Well, what say you to that? It seems as though we are both to see the mysterious duke – the *Beastly* Duke, as he is known, with our own eyes!"

Charlotte laughed and shook her head. "My dear Amelia, you are much too excited about this. The gentleman is called 'the Beastly Duke' for a reason and as father has reminded you, he is not in the least bit desirous of anyone else's company save but his own. You cannot be hopeful of receiving a warm welcome from him!"

Amelia smiled. "I do not know what sort of welcome we shall receive but if Lady Ashbourne has invited us, then I am certain he will not be able to say anything to turn us away."

"Though she does seem eager to introduce you to her son William." Charlotte lifted an eyebrow. "He is a Marquess, Amelia. Father would not have any difficulty in agreeing to such a match."

Amelia shook her head. "I do not think that father will be as eager to encourage a match between myself and anyone else, not when he has *you* and your marriage to Lord Stirling to think of. That must come first, before anything else."

Charlotte considered this as they walked into the dining room. "I am not certain that is so," she replied, sending a tingle up Amelia's spine. "You may find yourself not only meeting the mysterious 'Beastly Duke' but very soon thereafter, engaged to his brother! And then what shall you do?"

Trying to laugh along with her sister, Amelia's smile stuck but was not a true smile. The thought of being engaged to any gentleman, particularly one that her father might approve of but where she did not herself find their connection pleasing was a rather troubling one. Her sister might be contented with her circumstances but she herself would not be.

The thought of meeting the Beastly Duke, however, was an intriguing one and one that Amelia could not push from her mind. Meeting the Beastly Duke – under the premise of visiting his mother – meant that he would have no choice but to introduce himself and speak with them, would it not? An excited flicker caught Amelia's heart and she let out a slow breath, trying to keep herself composed. Her father's warning echoed in her mind, reminding her that the Beastly Duke might be just as he was described as being – beastly. He might well be rude, disinclined to their company and perhaps even refusing to come and greet them in the first place!

Amelia bit her lip, her thoughts in a whirlwind. The only way she was going to find out would be to visit the Ashbourne Estate which was going to come to her very soon indeed.

Chapter Four

Walking through the hall, Nathanial stopped suddenly as there came a knock to the door. Frowning, he glanced at the clock which stood above the front door, seeing it rather early for visitors.

The sound of footsteps told him that one of his staff was already coming towards the door, ready to answer it but Nathanial found himself stepping forward, going to the door before the footman could do so. Opening it, he stood framed in the doorway, in the space between the two young ladies who now stood on the doorstep and entrance to his own house.

"Might I be of aid to you?" His eyes narrowed a little. "This is no time for charity."

The two young ladies glanced at each other, with the second then frowning hard, her jaw pulling tight. Glittering green flickered in her eyes, her red curls escaping from either side of her bonnet. Nathanial's heart lurched though he ignored it immediately.

"We have not come to offer charity," the lady exclaimed, her cheeks now a little hotter. "We have an invitation."

Nathanial scowled, hating the interest that continued to push itself into his heart. The sooner he removed these young ladies from his company, the better. "I have not invited you."

"*You*?" The second young lady's eyes opened wide. "Are you the Beastly – I mean, are you the Duke of Ashbourne?"

"The very same." Aware that she had almost called him, 'The Beastly Duke', Nathanial's lip curled. "Though we are not acquainted so therefore, you cannot have been invited to this house."

Stepping back, he made to close the door only for the second young lady to step forward and, to his horror, pushing herself into the house. She came far too close to him for Nathanial's liking, a sweet scent catching his attention though he quickly flung it away.

"Whatever do you think you are doing?" he exclaimed, his fingers curling tightly as the first young lady stepped in also. "I shall have you flung from this house! How *dare* you – "

"Ashbourne! Whatever are you doing?"

Nathanial turned, his words cut off much too quickly as he saw his mother descending the staircase just behind him, her eyes round with shock. "Mother, these two young ladies have come into this house without warning and – "

"Lady Charlotte and Lady Amelia," his mother interrupted again, her tone dark. "The two young ladies I have invited here for the day. They will be staying with us for dinner before returning home."

Nathanial's shoulders dropped.

"My mother would like to express her profound apologies for not being able to join us," the second young lady said, taking a step closer to Lady Ashbourne. "She is greatly fatigued after recovering from a cold."

Lady Ashbourne's expression flickered with concern. "She is quite all right, I hope?"

"Yes, she is well recovered but in need of further rest." The first young lady bobbed a quick curtsy. "Thank you for your kind invitation. This is a beautiful home."

Nathanial scowled. He had no recollection of his mother informing him about such a thing but that did not mean that the lady had not done it. He might have been so distracted with his own thoughts and feelings that he had not given her the attention she deserved.

Frustration bit at him hard.

"I am sure that my son would be glad to show you about the house and the grounds."

Nathanial stiffened, his eyes searching his mother's face and seeing the glint in her eyes. "You shall have to forgive me. I have matters of business which cannot wait."

Lady Ashbourne frowned. "I do not think it is all that pressing, surely?"

"It is. My solicitor is already in my study, waiting for me." Making to walk past the two ladies, he stopped short when his mother spoke his name again.

"Ashbourne, you must permit me to introduce you properly to these two very fine young ladies. After all, that has not yet been done and we are all to sit to dinner together this evening!"

A curl of fire billowed in Nathanial's stomach but he forced himself to turn to the two young ladies. The second, the one who had pushed her way into the house, kept her chin lifted and her eyes sharp as he looked at her while the first had her eyes a little lowered, her face holding some color. Perhaps she was more embarrassed that the other.

"Might I present Lady Charlotte and Lady Amelia." His mother gestured to the first young lady, the one with her eyes lowered, and then to the second. "They are daughters to the Marquess of Stanton."

Understanding flared. "I see." Seeing his mother's eyes widen, Nathanial cleared his throat and bowed quickly, first to Lady Charlotte and then to Lady Amelia. "You are the ones who sent me the invitation to the literary event."

"Which *I* attended but you did not," his mother interjected as the second young lady nodded. "What a shame you did not feel as though it would be an enjoyable event, Ashbourne! It was very interesting indeed."

"I am sure it was." Gritting his teeth, Nathanial inclined his head and then stepped away. "I shall leave Lady Charlotte and Lady Amelia to your care, Mother." Making to stride away, he was forced to turn back when his mother called his name. "Yes?"

"You *will* be coming to join us this evening for dinner, I presume?" His mother's eyebrow arched, the tone of voice telling him that she would be most displeased if he were to refuse. "There was no argument from you yesterday when I spoke with you so there can be nothing today that would prevent you."

Nathanial tried to think of something – anything – that might have stepped in his way and thereafter, forced him back from dinner but nothing came to mind. Seeing the slight quirk on Lady Amelia's lips, he let out a frustrated sigh, having no concerns whatsoever about making his irritation known. "I do not think I can come up with anything to excuse myself, though I might well have wished it, so yes, Mother, I will join you for dinner."

A glimmer of a smile flew across Lady Ashbourne's face. "I suppose it must do, though I would have preferred a little more enthusiasm." Her chin lifted. "Enjoy the rest of your day, Ashbourne."

Without another word or even a smile in his mother's direction, Nathanial turned on his heel and marched towards his study, his jaw clenching tight. Part of him wanted to believe that his mother had orchestrated such a thing deliberately so that he would be forced into meeting Lady Charlotte and Lady Amelia but another part was frustrated with his own flickering interest in the ladies. As much as he tried to deny it, as much as he tried to pretend it was not there, that spark continued to fire through him. The scowl on his face lingered as he walked directly to his study, pushing the door open and seeing his solicitor rising to his feet almost immediately.

"Thank you for seeing me, Your Grace."

"But of course." Nathanial waved the man to sit back down. "We are to look at my current tenants, are we not?"

"Yes, that is so." The solicitor cleared his throat and then pulled out a pile of papers, setting them on Nathanial's desk. "I should say that most of your tenants are doing very well in terms of paying their rent. There is one family, however, who are in arrears."

Nathanial frowned. "By how much?"

A line formed across the solicitor's forehead. "They have not paid the rent in around eight months, Your Grace."

"And why is that?"

The man looked up at him for a moment and then dropped his head back to the papers. "It states that Mr. Brock has become severely unwell and is unable to work. His wife continues to care for him and does work where she can but it is a difficult situation."

Nathanial ran one hand over his chin. "Mr. Brock, does he seem to be making a recovery?"

"I do believe so, though from what the doctor has stated, it will be some time. I believe that the man fell from the roof, one that he had been thatching. His leg broke though it is already beginning to heal but he also endured a great and heavy fever which stole all of his strength. As I have said, there is illness and a lack of money in this particular situation, Your Grace, though they have not paid the rent as your other tenants have."

"Ah but they have not had the same difficulties either," Nathanial replied, slowly. "No, I will not force this family to pay the rent. The man was thatching a roof, you say?"

The solicitor nodded though Nathanial was certain he detected a slight hint of relief in the man's eyes. "The roof of another family," he told Nathanial. "It is his occupation, of course but on this occasion, he was fixing a hole in the roof of another tenant."

A kick hit Nathanial's heart. "Something that I myself ought to have been aware of and preparing for," he replied, a little heavily. "The houses and the roofs are my responsibility and this man was doing what was not required of him so that another tenant could be kept warm and dry. How wrong it would be for me to expect rent from such a family!"

His solicitor smiled.

"No, there shall be no rent expected until the man is able to begin work again and even then, he shall have another month's grace." Curling one hand into a fist, Nathanial set it down hard on the table. "In addition, make certain that this family has enough to eat. I presume there are children?"

Glancing at the papers, the solicitor nodded. "Three, Your Grace. The youngest is an infant."

Nathanial nodded slowly. "Then make certain there is enough food for that family. If the father cannot work and earn money and the mother has a young child dependent on her then what is she to do? Make certain that they know to come to you with any concerns or any lack. I will not have any one of my tenants suffering. Not if I can help it."

As he spoke, Nathanial's mind flashed back to Lady Amelia, though he could not understand why. He saw that wry smile that had danced across her lips when she had spoken to him, the sharpness in her eyes when she had looked at him. Did she think him an ogre? A man without kindness or consideration?

What does it matter what she thinks of me? he asked himself, as his solicitor continued to speak about the situation with the tenants. *I am to sit with them at the dinner table but that is all. Thereafter I shall not see them again and it means nothing to me what Lady Amelia thinks of either myself or my actions.* With a nod, he cleared his throat and then focused all of his attention upon his solicitor and pushed Lady Ameila from his mind.

Chapter Five

Sitting down to dinner with Lady Ashbourne was one thing but sitting down with the Beastly Duke was quite another. Amelia could not help but send glances in his direction every few minutes for, while the conversation at the dinner table was flowing rather well, the Duke had not said a single word thus far to any of them.

Amelia forced herself to focus on the conversation at hand, telling herself that there was nothing to be done other than to pay close attention to Lady Ashbourne so that she would not appear disinterested in what the lady had to say.

"Tell me about your betrothed, Lady Charlotte." Lady Ashbourne smiled as heat came into Charlotte's cheeks. "I have heard that he is an exceptional gentleman. Did you say that he hails from Scotland?"

Charlotte nodded though Amelia, again, threw a look to the Duke but the gentleman appeared much more interested in what was on his plate than what Charlotte was saying.

"Yes, he resides in Scotland. My father was very dear friends with his and therefore, there was always the hope that our two families would join in some way. I was not placed under any pressure to do so, however. It was always my choice."

"That was good of your father," Lady Ashbourne replied, gently. "I was not given any choice in the matter when it came to my own marriage. I was told only three weeks before the nuptials and everything was done for me. All I had to do was appear at the church, speak my promises and be contented with all that came to me thereafter." Her smile grew a little more. "Though I will admit to being very fortunate in the man I married. The Duke of Ashbourne was an excellent man and a kind-hearted one at that. He blessed us with two sons and a happy life which I admit, I did not expect. I do hope that you will have the very same blessing, Lady Charlotte."

"I thank you, Lady Ashbourne. I do admit to being a little anxious about it all but as I have said, I am certain that Lord Stirling is an excellent gentleman and therefore, I will be glad to marry him."

Lady Ashbourne nodded. "And what of you, Lady Amelia?"

Amelia blinked in surprise, remembering that she had already spoken to the lady of her situation and wondering why the lady asked her of it again – unless it was that she had forgotten the conversation between Amelia and herself at the literary event. "I am to go to London for my come out, I believe. My father spoke to me of it only yesterday."

The expression on Lady Ashbourne's face brightened. "Yes, I recall that now. So you are to go to London for the Season after all, then! I shall make certain to introduce you to William. He would be *very* glad to make your acquaintance I am sure." This was said with a swift glance towards the Duke of Ashbourne though, Amelia noted, the gentleman did not so much as flinch. Instead, he continued to eat calmly, though he did, at the very least, acknowledge his mother with a brief but tiny smile.

"I would be very glad to make his acquaintance," Amelia replied, quickly. "We are to depart next week, I believe. The weather has been so fine and my father does love the estate grounds so very much that it is a struggle for him to think of leaving for London!"

Lady Ashbourne laughed softly and picked up her wine glass. "I quite understand that. The weather has been – "

Before she could finish her sentence, such a loud crack of thunder ripped through the dining room that Amelia dropped her fork in shock. Lady Ashbourne gasped and even the Duke himself turned to look.

"A summer storm!" Lady Ashbourne exclaimed, as Amelia threw a look to Charlotte, seeing her sister's wide eyes. "Goodness and it is a severe one! I must admit, I was not expecting to see that!"

"Nor was I," Charlotte murmured, as Amelia swallowed tightly, recalling that they were soon to be departing for home and though the journey was not overly long, the drive through a summer storm would not be a pleasant one. She pressed her lips together, worry beginning to drive through her mind but, perhaps sensing Amelia's concern, Lady Ashbourne turned to her quickly.

"You will both have to stay until the morrow," she declared, though the Duke of Ashbourne immediately lifted his head, his eyes narrowing at his mother. "You cannot be sent home in a summer storm! Your parents will know that this is what has been decided, I am sure, though I can send a message to them if you would prefer."

Amelia looked to Charlotte but Charlotte immediately shook her head. "Pray, do not. I am certain my mother and father will understand where we are and what has happened. No doubt they will have been taken by surprise by this storm, just as we have been!"

Lady Ashbourne nodded. "Very good. I will have rooms prepared for you both and you need not worry, there will be a few spare night things for your comfort also. I always keep many things for times such as this!"

"Thank you, Your Grace. You are very kind." Amelia smiled at the lady, only for the Duke himself to interrupt.

"It may be over very quickly," he said, as rain began to hit hard at the windows, followed by another crack of thunder which made Amelia start violently. "You may find yourselves able to return home just as you had anticipated."

Amelia did not know what to say, looking from the Duke to Lady Ashbourne – who had gone rather red in the face – to Charlotte, who was now looking down at her plate.

"I... I apologise."

Looking up, Amelia took in the rather red face of the Duke of Ashbourne, seeing the look of regret on his face, his eyes darting from place to place as though he had only just realized what he had said.

"Your safety and comfort is of the greatest priority, of course." Clearing his throat, the Duke gestured to them both. "Forgive my hasty speech. I assume that you will both desire to return home as planned but as my mother has said, we are more than able to accommodate you here."

"Thank you, Your Grace." Amelia kept her gaze steady, looking at him. "I think it would be wise for us both to remain here overnight, if the storm continues to rage. The roads have been very dry certainly but they can easily become very muddy very quickly."

"You are quite correct, Lady Amelia." Lady Ashbourne looked again at her son, her gaze hard, before she smiled in Amelia's direction. "Of course you must both stay here. I will have the servants prepare rooms for you both at once." Clicking to the waiting footman, she quickly gave them directions as Amelia looked to Charlotte, seeing how her sister caught her lip between her teeth for a moment, clearly a little anxious.

"Mayhap a message might be sent to my parents, if it would not be too much trouble. I am certain they would be glad to have whoever you send reside there until the storm is over." Amelia looked to Lady Ashbourne who nodded quickly. "It would bring relief to my mother's mind, I am sure, to know that we intend to reside there."

The Duke coughed. "I could ride, I am sure."

"Pray, do not think that you must go yourself, Your Grace," Amelia replied, quickly. "I do not wish to trouble you. If you do not think it wise for any of your servants to be sent out in this weather then I am sure my mother and father will understand what has happened."

"I will send a footman," Lady Ashbourne said, before her son could speak though Amelia caught the way the Duke's jaw tightened. He was, she thought, attempting to be respectful by not speaking over or against his mother though, no doubt, he would have liked to have had what *he* had decided to be the way forward. In a way, Amelia considered, she respected him in that though she was still rather displeased with the obvious way he had suggested Charlotte and she might still return home this evening.

"Thank you, Your Grace." Charlotte now looked a good deal less concerned, her smile returning. "Your kindness is greatly appreciated."

"But of course." Lady Ashbourne gestured to them both. "Now, let us all enjoy our dinner and thereafter, there will be cards and tea in the drawing room. What say you to that?"

Amelia, who had enjoyed a very nice afternoon in Lady Ashbourne's company, for the lady was both easy to speak with and never short of conversation, found herself smiling, relaxing now despite the storm outside. "I think that would be lovely, Your Grace." Turning her head, her heart jolted as the Duke scowled, though he quickly pushed it from his features when he caught her eye. "And you, Your Grace, will you be joining us?"

His tight smile did not offer Amelia any sense of pleasure in her question. "Alas, Lady Amelia, I shall not be joining you. I am afraid that I have matters of business to attend to."

"I see." Amelia did not return his smile but instead, simply looked at him for a moment longer before taking her attention back to her dinner. This was a very strange circumstance, she considered, though she was glad to be kept safe from the summer storm. Staying at the Beastly Duke's estate was certainly unexpected and from the way he continued to scowl, Amelia was sure he had no desire for them to linger.

"What do you think of him, then?"

Amelia smiled as she sat down on the edge of her bed, looking across at Charlotte. "Of the Beastly Duke?"

Charlotte nodded. "Yes, what do you think of him? I myself must confess that the term, 'Beastly Duke' does seem to fit his demeanor. Did you see how eager he was for us to consider returning home?" She gestured to the window. "Even though the storm rages? Even though the lightning and thunder still rolls above us?"

"He did apologise for that, however," Amelia replied, gently. "Let us not criticize him for that. Though yes, I will admit that I was displeased with how eager he seemed to have us removed from his house."

Charlotte sighed and shook her head. "He does not seem to be pleased by anything. Talk of London and society did not bring a smile to his lips. Whatever we spoke of, all he did was sit and look down at his plate and paid us very little attention."

"Not that I gave that much attention, given just how conversational Lady Ashbourne was." Amelia smiled as Charlotte laughed softly, her ire gone in a moment.

"Yes, she is quite lovely. I think her a very dear lady and I should be glad to be in her company whenever she might wish it. It is very good for her to invite us here, though I do think that she might have another thought as to why she has done that."

"And what is that?"

Charlotte's eyebrow lifted. "Because she wishes to introduce you to her son."

Immediately, Amelia laughed and shook her head, believing that her sister was doing nothing but teasing her. "I am to be introduced to William, the younger brother, remember? The Beastly Duke is certainly *not* inclined towards meeting me or any other young lady I should imagine!"

"All the same," Charlotte replied, slowly, "I am sure that the lady intended to see what her son's reaction would be to your presence."

"What about you? Why could it not be that you... oh." Amelia's shoulders dropped. "You are engaged, of course." Frowning, she gave another toss of her head. "No, I am sure that there is nothing in that whatsoever. Lady Ashbourne wishes to introduce me to her *younger* son, something I am not at all disinclined to, I must admit! So long he is not as sour a character as his brother!"

Charlotte giggled. "I am sure that his brother cannot be as beastly as the Duke of Ashbourne. You may find yourself quite taken with the gentleman! Could you imagine being wed to the Marquess but having the Beastly Duke for a brother?"

"I could not." Amelia gave a slight shudder. "The Beastly Duke does not appear to have enjoyment in anything! To have his dark and grave character sitting over us would not be something pleasing, I must confess."

"Indeed. Though his estate and the grounds are very pleasing."

Amelia smiled. "Yes, I will admit to that. The gardens especially are very lovely. You know how much I delight in walking through beautiful grounds."

"I do." Charlotte grinned. "You must hope that William's estate has the most remarkable gardens also else you shall always be pining for *these* grounds, I fear."

Laughing again, Amelia chose not to rise to her sister's teasing and instead made her way across the room so she might begin her ministration before taking to bed. It had been a most unexpected circumstance to remain in the Duke of Ashbourne's estate overnight but she certainly did not mind lingering in such a beautiful house for a little longer... though she was not looking forward to being in the Duke of Ashbourne's company come the morning!

***

Lighting the candle, Amelia made her way to the door, her heart pounding. She had woken suddenly, sure she had heard

32

something but being entirely uncertain as to what it was. Rather than lingering in her bed, however, she had decided to rise, just to prove to herself that there was nothing wrong so she might return to an easy sleep again.

The door clicked open and as she pulled it back, another sound ran towards her, making her skin prickle. It sounded, to her mind, as though someone was shouting but given that there was only the Duke of Ashbourne and Lady Ashbourne in the house, surely it could not be either of them? It was much too early for anyone to rise for, glancing at the window, Amelia saw only the very first fingers of dawn had begun to spread across the sky.

"No! *No!*"

She stopped, her heart thudding furiously in her chest as she waited, fearing that something more would come. It sounded as though someone was in trouble, as though they were fighting back against something or someone though Amelia could not hear anyone else. Glancing behind her, Amelia wondered whether or not she ought to return to her bed but hearing the shout again, forced her feet forward. If someone was in difficulty, if there was something she could do to help, then she would not lack courage and return to her chamber.

Without warning, the sound of a door slamming back against the wall made her jump, only for stumbling footsteps to rush towards her. Letting out a shriek of fright, Amelia fell back against the wall as a figure came to a stop in front of her. The light from her candle lit his features and, her heart still pounding, Amelia looked back into the face of the Duke of Ashbourne.

His dark hair was messy, his eyes wild, searching her face as if he was trying to place her. His night shirt gaped open, his hands reaching out to her and though she was not afraid of him, Amelia shrank back.

"Lady... Lady Amelia." The Duke's voice was hoarse, his eyes squeezing closed as he dragged in a long breath. "Forgive me. I... "

His hand found hers and though Amelia expected him to pull his hand away immediately, his fingers wound through hers and he pressed them hard as though she was the anchor he needed to hold him steady in this dark situation.

"Forgive me," he said again, his voice now a little steadier, a little firmer. "I have dreams which terrify me on occasion and I find myself lost within them."

"I heard your shouts and thought someone was in trouble." Amelia let out a slow breath, trying to slow her heart to a steady rhythm again. "Are you quite all right?"

The Duke of Ashbourne nodded and then looked down to where their hands were joined. He quickly let her go, pulling his hand away and then putting both hands behind his back, clearing his throat gruffly and turning his head away. "Do excuse me. You should return to your room now, Lady Ameila. I am quite all right, as you can see."

She nodded and turned away wordlessly, her other hand gripping the candlestick as she hurried back along the hallway to her room. She glanced behind her, seeing the Duke of Ashbourne still standing there, looking back at her and a slight shiver ran down her spine. There were a good many questions in her mind, questioning what it was the Duke had been dreaming about, what had scared him so much that he had run from his room and into the hallway but she kept those questions to herself. It would do no good to speak with him for she did not have any expectation that he would answer! With a small sigh, Amelia stepped back into her bedchamber and, setting the candle down, leaned back against the door and closed her eyes.

It was only then she realized just how much she was trembling.

Chapter Six

"Good morning, Lady Amelia, Lady Charlotte." Not quite able to meet Lady Amelia's eye, Nathanial bowed and then sat down quickly. "I do hope you both slept well."

It was not a question but rather a statement and as Nathanial reached for the coffee, he saw the two ladies glance at each other. No doubt Lady Amelia had already told her sister of what had happened and that embarrassed him all the more. It had been that foolish dream which had woken him, that nightmare that would not leave him. Somehow, he had found himself out in the hallway, his bare feet cold on the floor as he searched for William, only to come back to himself and realize that he was now clutching a hold of Lady Amelia's hand. He had been unable to pull his hand away either, looking at her with wide eyes, his heart thudding furiously as he slowly began to calm himself. There had been something about the way he had taken her hand which had brought him a greater comfort than he had ever experienced before. He could not explain it, not even now as he sat at the dining table in their company, but it had been there, nonetheless. It had quietened his fractious mind, steadied his furiously beating heart and had let a slow relief begin to course through him. It had brought him back to the present rather than letting him linger in that dream which had caused him so much torment.

"Good morning, Lady Amelia, Lady Charlotte!"

With a trill, Nathanial's mother made her way into the drawing room, waving for the two ladies to remain seated rather than rise to greet her. "I do hope you are rested?"

"Yes, very well rested, I thank you." Lady Amelia spoke clearly, not so much as glancing towards Nathanial. "The summer storm seems to have dissipated entirely!"

Nathanial's gaze went to the windows, taking in the beautiful summer morning. Sunlight was streaming through the windows and the rain, thunder and lightning which had been heavy on them last evening was nothing more than a faint memory.

"I will have your carriage prepared once you have eaten your fill," Lady Ashbourne replied, sitting herself down. "I am sure your parents will want to have you back with them."

"I thank you." The smile on Lady Amelia's face was one of relief and Nathanial immediately frowned, wondering if this was due to his own strange behavior toward her last evening. He already had the name, 'the Beastly Duke', did he want Lady Amelia to spread yet more whispers about him? A sudden fear began to wrap around his mind, telling him that even though he had no intention of going to London for the Season, if Lady Amelia was to go as she had indicated, then she would start telling every one of her friends precisely what had happened. The *ton* would mock him, no doubt, spreading yet more whispers about his character, adding a heavier weight to the title of, 'the Beastly Duke' and leaving him without any comfort whatsoever.

I must speak with her.

"You say you are both to go to London this Season?"

Both Lady Charlotte and Lady Amelia looked towards him at once, surprise glittering in their eyes though Lady Amelia was the first to answer.

"Yes, Your Grace. We are."

"Why do you ask?" Lady Ashbourne poured herself a cup of tea, looking over at him as she set the teapot down. "You have not thought to go to London yourself, have you?"

Nathanial coughed and looked away. "I – I am no longer as certain as I was, Mama. It may be that I decide to make my way to town after all." He looked again to Lady Amelia, seeing the way her eyebrows lifted in obvious surprise. "I have not decided as yet."

"I see." There was a slight hint of triumph in Lady Ashbourne's voice though Nathanial steadfastly ignored it. "I am certain that both William and myself would be very glad to have you join us there."

Nathanial nodded and picked up a piece of toast. "I should like to see my brother again, as you well know, Mother," he said, making it quite clear – he hoped – that this was not to do with Lady Amelia's presence. "I was thinking on this last evening. If he is *not* to come home to the estate – or if he is to stay only briefly – then that shall not satisfy me. I must go and spend time with him where he is. Namely, in London."

"As I have said, I am sure your brother would be very glad to see you." Lady Ashbourne looked again to Lady Amelia. "When is it that you will be leaving for London, do you know?"

Lady Amelia smiled. "I believe by the end of the month, Lady Ashbourne."

"Capital. Then we shall see each other very often in London, I am sure." Lady Ashbourne smiled and sent the glowing look in Nathanial's direction though he looked away. "Now then, let us finish breaking our fast and we will have you prepared for home."

***

"Lady Amelia, might I speak with you for a moment?" Nathanial folded his arms across his chest as Lady Amelia jumped in surprise, then turned to look at him directly. He had stepped out from a corner in the library where the young lady had unexpectedly come in, evidently not quite ready to depart as yet.

"Your Grace." She inclined her head. "Do excuse me, the carriage is not yet ready and – "

"Might I speak with you?"

The lady lifted her chin and looked back at him, perhaps determined not to show him that she held any fear in her heart over his presence. "Yes, if you wish."

"The door is ajar and you may escape whenever you wish," Nathanial said, gesturing to it. "I come to speak with you about last evening."

Lady Amelia let her gaze settle on his, a steadiness in her eyes that he had not expected. "I do not think that there is anything that needs to be said, Your Grace. It is clear that you found great distress in your dreams."

"I did not – " Stopping himself, Nathanial closed his eyes briefly. "Yes, I suppose that is true. If I am to be truthful, I would tell you that I often have dreams which can be rather unsettling. It was not simply because your sister and you had resided here or because of the storm." A little uncertain as to why he said such a thing, he quickly cleared his throat and lifted his shoulders, letting them fall quickly. "I apologise that you saw me in such difficulty."

The edge of Lady Amelia's lips curved. "Your Grace, there is nothing for you to apologise for. You were asleep, as you said. Therefore, why would you apologise for that? It was not as though you could be freed from your dream nor could you be responsible for what happened."

37

"But you were a little alarmed."

Her smile grew softly. "Yes, I admit that I was. However, when I saw that you were in distress, my concern for you grew rather than being concerned for myself. I am only glad that you recovered quickly and that I was able to help you in a small way."

Nathanial cleared his throat, now feeling a little disconcerted as he remembered how he had taken her hand and the comfort that had brought him. Was she thinking of the same thing?

"It is just as well you will not see me in such a state again," he muttered, passing one hand over his eyes and recalling what it was that he wanted to say to her in the first place. "However, now that I know you are to go to London and that all of society will be there, I must ask you if you might be willing not to speak of this to anyone else."

The moment he said it, Nathanial grew concerned that he had made some dreadful mistake. Lady Amelia's eyes grew wide only for her then to frown, her hands going to her waist, her elbows akimbo.

"Your Grace, I am deeply offended that you think I am some sort of gossip!"

"It is not that, Lady Amelia," he said, quickly, only for her to interrupt him, her eyes blazing with indignation now.

"I am not the sort of person who would *ever* spread rumours about you or anyone else," she exclaimed, her voice growing in strength. "You might not be aware of my character given that you have never *once* come to call, nor have accepted any invitations which have been sent to you but had you done so, then you might now be aware that I am not in the *least* bit inclined towards any sort of gossip. I despise it. I think it the very worst thing of all. I should not like to have a word of rumour spoken about me and therefore, I would not be willing to speak a word of it about anyone else! What sort of person would I be if I willingly laughed and spoke about a gentleman's distress? A distress known solely to himself and something that, I am sure, you are eager to keep entirely to yourself! I am not unaware of such things, Your Grace nor am I unsympathetic to them. So no, you need not have any concern. I will not say a word about this to anyone. The only person I have spoken to of it and *will* speak to of it is my sister, Lady Charlotte."

Nathanial took her in, seeing her flushed cheeks and the flash of ire in her eyes and felt himself a little embarrassed. Mayhap this ought to have been only a brief word to her rather than a prolonged conversation – or mayhap he ought not to have said anything at all. "I did not mean to upset you, Lady Amelia. As you know, I do not know you at all and therefore, I wanted to make certain that it would not occur." Wincing, he looked away from her piercing gaze. "I have enough of a reputation already. Do not think I am unaware of it."

There came then a silence which Nathanial could not speak into. He could not seem to find the words to speak into the quiet and nor could he bring himself to look at the lady. This was an awkwardness such as he had never experienced before and it was, he recognized, entirely of his own making.

"You are aware that you are referred to as..." Lady Amelia closed her eyes. "Forgive me. I did not mean to say – "

"I am 'the beastly Duke', am I not?" With a sad smile, Nathanial finally caught Lady Amelia's eye again. "Yes, I will admit that I am all too aware of that name, Lady Amelia. My own mother has informed me of it for she is entirely displeased by the name though I do not particularly mind."

Lady Amelia's eyes rounded. "You are not concerned about being called such a thing?"

His shoulders lifted. "No, I am not. I am not in society so it does not matter to me what is being said of me. Yes, I am a gentleman inclined to his own company. I am also aware that my disposition being what it is, I am then given this specific name but what can be done about it? I have no inclination to change it nor do I have any interest in returning to society and having them learn about my character. So though I am aware of it, yes, I have no interest in altering it. However, nor do I wish anything to be added to it."

"I quite understand." Lady Amelia smiled and, much to Nathanial's surprise, reached out and touched his hand. It was only brief but heat spiraled up through his arm and into his heart, making it quicken. "I do apologise for being a little curt, Your Grace. Please, have every reassurance that I will not speak a word of this to anyone. And Charlotte, I can promise you, is also just as discreet as I."

He nodded, a little disappointed when her hand left his. "Thank you, Lady Amelia. I hope your return drive home is a pleasant one."

She smiled and then left his presence without a word, the door closing tight behind her as Nathanial fought the strange and compelling urge to rush after her. There was something about Lady Amelia's presence that he did not like for it disconcerted him in a way that he had never experienced before. Pushing that from his mind, he focused instead on the relief that came with the knowledge that what had taken place between them would remain quite secret.

Though, he considered, going to settle himself in a comfortable chair, he might still make his way to London for the Season regardless.

Chapter Seven

One month later.

"Your come out was quite lovely. You did very well."

Amelia smiled at her sister. "It was not as difficult as I feared it would be. All that was required was a curtsy, a brief smile and then that was it at its end!"

"Yes but for many, the thought of curtsying before the King himself is a heavy weight upon their mind!"

Amelia laughed softly, relieved that it was over. "I confess that I did find myself a little anxious, fearful that I would fall over as I curtsied or that, indeed, it would not be correct. I am glad now that it is at an end."

Charlotte smiled. "And now all you need to worry about is your debut ball! You look ready, however. More than that, you look quite beautiful."

Smiling, Amelia took in her reflection as she looked in the full length mirror. She was wearing a cream gown which had lace at the sleeves. Long, silk gloves came just above her elbows and pearls were threaded through her hair. Diamonds danced at her ears and her cheeks were already flushed simply by the excitement which ran through her. Yes, she considered, she was looking well, certainly but she was herself a little nervous.

Will the Beastly Duke be present?

Where that thought had come from, Amelia was not certain but the moment it entered her mind, heat rushed through her with such force, it quite took her breath away.

"Are you quite all right?"

Charlotte was at her elbow and Amelia pushed the thought away quickly, turning to smile at her sister. "Yes, I am quite well. I will not pretend that I am not a little nervous, however."

"There is nothing to be concerned about," Charlotte insisted, quickly. "All you must do is dance and then smile at every gentleman who wishes to dance with you. Make some light conversation, greet new acquaintances with decorum and all will be well. Who knows? You may be considered a diamond of the first water!"

Amelia laughed and shook her head. "I have no need to be considered as a diamond. All I wish for is to be seen just as I am and for any new acquaintances to think well of me. I do not want gentlemen to seek me out because they think me handsome enough for them!"

Charlotte laughed and made to say something more, only for their mother to open the door and come inside. She gasped, her hands flying to her mouth as she took in Amelia's appearance and such was her delight, tears began to burn in her eyes.

"You look quite lovely, my dear." Lady Stanton came closer, her hands going out towards Amelia. "How wonderful it is as a mother to see you now presented to society. I am sure you will do *very* well."

"Thank you, Mama."

Lady Stanton took in a breath and squeezed Amelia's hands. "I have received a note from Lady Ashbourne. She writes to tell me that she will be present this evening and would be very glad to introduce you to her younger son."

Amelia's heart flipped over in her chest. "Yes, she did say such a thing when we visited her. He is a Marquess, I believe."

"Yes, the Marquess of Highcroft. He seems to be a gentleman with an excellent reputation, who has the *ton* speaking well of him and a kindness about him which is a wonderful thing to hear about any gentleman, I must say." Lady Stanton's eyes flickered as Amelia smiled. "You might find yourself interested in him, my dear."

"I might, Mama," Amelia admitted, though for whatever reason, the Duke of Ashbourne immediately came into her mind. "Though I shall not make any judgements about any gentleman, not when I am only just about to make my own debut."

Lady Stanton laughed. "Very wise, my dear," she answered, releasing Amelia's hands. "Now, shall we make to the carriage? If you are ready, then we should take our leave."

Amelia nodded and then let out a slow breath, surprised at how suddenly anxious she was. Whether it came from knowing that she was to attend her very first ball as a debutante or because of Lady Ashbourne's presence – as well as her potential introduction to the Marquess of Highcroft – she could not say. Try as she might, however, she could not rid herself of her nerves as

42

she made her way alongside Charlotte to the carriage and onward to the ball.

* * *

"Good evening, Lady Amelia. How very glad I am to see you again!"

Amelia smiled and dropped into a curtsy. "Good evening, Your Grace. I am very pleased to see you. I do hope you have been enjoying the London Season thus far?"

Lady Ashbourne's eyes sparkled as she smiled, making it appear to Amelia that she was enjoying the Season almost as much as Amelia herself!

"It is an excellent Season thus far, I must say. I have been delighted to spend time in my younger son's company, for he has spent many years at Eton and the last few years, settled in his own estate and I do miss his company a great deal." She smiled at Amelia and then looked to Charlotte. "And is your betrothed to come to London?"

"I have had a letter stating that he hopes to be here within the month," Charlotte replied, her own smile growing as Amelia watched, knowing that her sister and Lord Stirling had been exchanging letters for some time now and wondering to herself if these letters had built an affection for Lord Stirling in her sister's heart. "I do look forward to seeing him again."

"That is good. Ah, and there is your own dear mother!"

Amelia stepped to one side as Lady Ashbourne greeted Lady Stanton warmly, glad that the ball was going so well at this present moment. Yes, she had been nervous but after one promenade around the ballroom, she found herself less anxious and, thereafter, had been delighted to see Lady Ashbourne again. There were more than a few acquaintances that Amelia had been able to greet and while there would be many new acquaintances to be introduced to, she had enough friends to keep her contented.

"Now, would you permit me to introduce you all to my younger son? Since you have all met my eldest, it would be a great honour for me to introduce Highcroft to you all."

"But of course!" Amelia's mother exclaimed, her delight obvious as she glanced to Amelia, a small smile touching the corners of her mouth. "Is he present this evening?"

"He is." Lady Ashbourne waved one hand. "If you will excuse me for just a moment, I will fetch him."

Amelia stood quietly, watching as Lady Ashbourne stepped away. Charlotte and their mother immediately began to converse but Amelia herself stood silently, taking in the many gentlemen and ladies present within the ballroom. Her gaze shifted slowly around the room – only to snag and then to stop on one particular gentleman.

The Beastly Duke.

His eyes flared and then centered on her again, his jaw tightening, his shoulders straightening as he slowly inclined his head. Not knowing what to do, Amelia held his gaze for a moment or two longer and then, with a brief nod, turned her head away entirely. It felt as though every part of her was burning, heat flaring through her as she felt her skin prickling, wondering now if the Beastly Duke was continuing to study her even though she was not looking at him.

"Thank you for your patience." Lady Ashbourne reappeared, a gentleman beside her though Amelia quickly took in that he had a slight limp though it did not appear to affect him too greatly. It was only that he appeared somewhat stiff in his gait. "My dear friends, permit me to introduce my son, the Marquess of Highcroft. Highcroft, this is Lady Stanton, married to the Marquess of Stanton and their daughters, Lady Charlotte – now engaged to the Marquess of Stirling – and Lady Amelia."

Lord Highcroft immediately dropped into a bow but when he lifted his head, there was a light smile on his face which Amelia felt lift her heart. He had the same blue eyes as his brother but they were warm rather than cold and the dark hair on his head was a shade lighter than that of the Beastly Duke. It was his smile, however, which she felt altered him so significantly from his brother. It lifted his entire expression, sent light into his face and made her feel as though he were glad to be introduced to them all. How different this was from the Beastly Duke!

"I am delighted to make your acquaintance, though I am sure that we were introduced to each other as children at some point."

Amelia laughed as he smiled back at her. "No doubt, Lord Highcroft, though I confess I do not remember it."

"Nor I. Therefore, we must pretend that this is our first meeting then, yes?" That smile had grown to a grin. "My mother informs me that this is your debut ball, Lady Amelia. Is it going well?"

A slight flush touched Amelia's cheeks. "Thus far, yes. I have been glad to greet some old acquaintances and there are many here that I must still be introduced to!"

"And your dance card is quickly being filled, I hope?" He smiled and held out one hand. "Though if there is any space, I should be glad to take one."

Amelia blinked, a little surprised at how quickly he had changed the topic of conversation. "You should like to dance with me?"

He nodded. "If I can." Turning to Charlotte, he smiled at her. "And you also, Lady Charlotte, if you would be willing to stand up with me?"

"I am sure that both my daughters would be very glad to do so." Lady Stanton threw a quick look towards Amelia who, still a little surprised, took the dance card from her wrist and offered it to Lord Highcroft. The gentleman smiled, thanked her and perused it quickly.

"If you might be willing, brother, I will take the dance cards thereafter."

A streak of astonishment had Amelia's breath hitching as she turned her head to see none other than the Duke of Ashbourne himself had come to join them, though he had come from behind them all so she had not seen him approach.

"That is, should you both be willing to permit me to stand up with you." The Duke cleared his throat and put his hands behind his back. "It is entirely up to you."

Lady Stanton laughed though the sound was a little forced. "Your Grace! Of course, my daughters would be delighted to stand up with you."

"Of course," Amelia murmured, as Charlotte did the same. The truth was – though the Duke was entirely unaware of her feelings, of course – she felt herself rather nervous at the thought of dancing with him, though at the same time, a little excited. A sudden recollection of how his hand had felt on hers flew right back into her mind and she caught her breath suddenly, turning her face away so that no-one would catch the way her face flushed.

This was the most extraordinary feeling to be having and try as she might, Amelia could not seem to rid herself of it. What was it about this Beastly Duke that so intrigued her? The man was of a sour disposition, his expressions always dark and his welcome to her less than warm and yet, for whatever reason, her interest in him was continuing to burgeon.

"The quadrille, Lady Amelia." Lord Highcroft smiled and then handed the card to his brother, though he did not even glance at him as he did so. "And Lady Charlotte, might I take the country dance?"

"I would be very glad if you did, my lord," Charlotte replied, as Amelia looked back steadily at the Duke of Ashbourne, wondering what it was that he intended to take from *her* dance card. She had not yet been granted permission to waltz so it could not be that... though the thought of dancing with the Duke, of finding herself close to him was a rather absorbing thought.

"Then I shall take the country dance for Lady Amelia," the Duke intoned, sounding less than interested in standing up with her even though he had been the one to ask it. "And then Lady Charlotte, the quadrille. That way, my brother and I will dance with each of you in turn."

"A capital idea!" Lady Ashbourne looked absolutely delighted and despite her strange considerations of the Duke of Ashbourne, Amelia could not help but smile in return. "Now, Lady Amelia, you must go and speak to as many of these acquaintances as you can – and make as many *new* acquaintances as you wish! Now that you have both the Marquess of Highcroft and the Duke of Ashbourne on your dance card, society will certainly take notice of you – as well they should! A beautiful, charming lady such as yourself ought to have all of society looking upon her. I am sure that many a gentleman will be glad to have his name upon your dance card."

"You are very kind, Lady Ashbourne." Seeing the Duke handing her back the dance card, Amelia reached out to take it, only to pull her hand back as their fingers brushed. It was as though she had been scalded, as though some red, hot heat had burned through her and the shock of it made her drop the dance card completely.

The Duke cleared his throat and then quickly bent to pick it up. "Do excuse me." The second time he held it out to her, Amelia – though already embarrassed – took it by the ribbon so she would not risk touching his fingers again and then slipped it upon her wrist.

A quick glance around the group told her that no-one else had noticed her reaction and, thus relieved, she let out a slow breath of relief.

"I look forward to our dance, Your Grace. And to yours also, Lord Highcroft." Charlotte bobbed her head and Amelia did the same before being taken from their company and led away to meet yet more acquaintances – though Amelia could not help but glance over her shoulder to once more look to the Duke... though he himself had already turned away.

***

"There is not much time for conversation during the quadrille, I am afraid." Amelia tried to smile, tried to speak as her heart thudded lightly – both from exertion and from the anxiousness which filled her at being in the Duke of Ashbourne's company. "Though there can still be a little."

The Duke sniffed and turned away as the steps led them through the dance. When they were next able to speak, his blue eyes caught hers for a moment and then looked away from her again.

Amelia's spirits sank. The Duke either regretted offering to dance with her or he was only doing so out of obligation. Mayhap his mother had urged him to do so. Mayhap since his brother was to do so, he felt himself compelled to do the same. Either way, he did not seem to be at all interested in conversing with her.

47

I was foolish to find myself intrigued by this gentleman, she told herself as they continued to dance in silence. *I shall dismiss him from my thoughts and vow not to ponder upon his existence any further.*

The dance continued and though Amelia tried again to make conversation, the Duke of Ashbourne responded only with a few brief words or with merely a nod. When it came to a close, he stepped back, bowed and then offered her his arm without a word, ready to take her back to her mother.

"I do not enjoy dancing… or conversing with banality, Lady Amelia," he said, making her head lift sharply, his words piercing her as though *she* had been somehow foolish in attempting to speak with him. "Mayhap you ought to tell your sister that so that she does not have the same expectations as you."

Heat burned a line up Amelia's spine, her face growing hot as anger tightened her core. "Your Grace, it is expected for a gentleman and lady to converse where possible. I do not think it wrong to have such expectations. Rather, I think it rude that a gentleman refuses to do so!"

"Is that so?" the Duke responded, mildly, sniffing and turning his head away. He said nothing more, not until he had brought her back to her mother. With a nod, the Duke released her arm and without so much as a final glance in her direction, turned on his heel and walked away.

Chapter Eight

"Lady Charlotte and Lady Amelia are both very pleasant, are they not?"

Nathanial looked at his brother, trying to ascertain if he meant anything more in expressing that aloud, though William merely smiled and continued his way across the room. Was it just Nathanial's eyes or was William's limp a little more pronounced today?

Nathanial's stomach twisted. As glad as he was to be in his brother's company again, there was always that awareness of his brother's injury and with that awareness, a renewing of Nathanial's guilt.

"Yes, it is a little worse today but that is only because I danced very often last evening."

Jerking in surprise, Nathanial's gaze flew up to his brother's face but William was smiling gently, his shoulders lifting.

"I can see you looking at me and I know that you continually are filled with concern, though I wish you would not worry," he told Nathanial quietly. "I am quite well and, as you can see, more than able to walk and dance as required."

"Though it costs you."

William chuckled. "I do not see that as a particular difficulty, brother. Dancing with various pretty young ladies is well worth the pain that might follow thereafter!"

Nathanial swallowed, not smiling. "I wish that I had never brought about this situation with your leg."

William's smile faded, his eyebrows lifting. "Brother, this was many years ago! Why would you let such a thing trouble you now?"

"Because... because I see the evidence of my foolishness and my neglect," Nathanial replied, turning his head away so that he would not have to look into his brother's eyes. "I wish it were not so."

There came then a small, short silence and Nathanial could barely glance at his brother, his guilt overwhelming him to the point that he fought to keep his heart steady.

"Ashbourne." William's voice had dropped a little lower, a heaviness there which had not been present before. "I do not hold this against you so why must you continually hold this pain against your heart? It was not just you who was foolish in that situation. I also was ridiculous in my actions."

"You were but a child!"

"As were you," William put in, quickly. "Come now, brother, do not hold any sort of guilt next to your heart for I certainly do not!"

"I do not see how you cannot."

William spread his hands out. "Because I was young and foolish and you were young and foolish. I am grateful for my life, Ashbourne. There is nothing about this life that troubles me for I know full well that I might not have *had* this life, had things been different! My leg aches a little and yes, I limp on occasion but that does not mean that it causes me any great difficulty. Do not let this trouble you, Ashbourne, I beg you. Not any longer."

Nathanial took in a deep breath, a little surprised at how his skin prickled at his brother's words. He waited to see if the guilt would fade from him but though it lessened a little, it still lingered, clinging to him with greater strength. "You say you danced with many a young lady last evening?" he asked, changing the subject completely. "But you thought Lady Charlotte and Lady Amelia the most delightful?"

"I did not say delightful but yes, I suppose that they are."

"You are aware that the eldest is already engaged?"

"Yes, to Lord Stirling. I am already acquainted with that gentleman, actually." William grinned. "He is an excellent fellow, though I should not like to live in Scotland!"

Nathanial chuckled. "It seems that Lady Charlotte does not care about such things, given that she has agreed to marry him."

"Though Lady Amelia is not engaged?"

Nathanial shook his head, aware of the streak which ran straight up his spine – though he did not permit it to flare in his heart as it wished to do.

"She told me that I was a good deal more conversational that you, however." William tilted his head as Nathanial shot him a quick look. "You did not speak with her during the dance?"

"Speak?" Nathanial shook his head. "No, I did not. Why ever should I do so? Dancing is not the time for conversation."

"Of course it is!" William threw up his hands. "If there is time to converse during the dance then gentlemen ought to make most of such an opportunity. Why would they not?"

Nathanial sighed and waved one hand. "Because it is banal conversation which holds no interest for me. I have no desire to talk about the weather or family or whether or not I am enjoying the Season."

"And what if the lady you dance with desires such a thing?"

Nathanial rolled his eyes. "Then I am afraid they will not be given what they are looking for, not from me."

"And this is why your reputation will continue to be dark and displeasing." With a sigh, William sank down into his chair. "Do you enjoy being known as 'the Beastly Duke'?"

Nathanial's jaw tightened. "I do not care for whispers and rumours either, brother."

"It is not a rumour nor a whisper," his brother contented. "Rather, it is a name which is stuck to you and you seem to be making no attempts to remove it from yourself."

"And do you think that I could?"

William nodded quickly, a light flickering in his eyes. "Of course you could. Instead of appearing dark and despondent, you must appear bright and happy!"

Nathanial's lip curled but his brother only laughed.

"That is not exactly the expression I was hoping to see upon your face, brother!"

"I am perfectly contented as I am," Nathanial replied, keeping his expression just as it was. "I do not feel the need to change."

"Are you certain?" William lifted an eyebrow. "How ever are you to get the attention of a young lady if you continue to be so disgruntled?"

Nathanial opened his mouth to state that he had no intention of catching the attention of a young lady, only to see the glint in his brother's eyes and choosing instead to say nothing whatsoever. He was not interested in any young lady, he told himself. There was no young lady which caught his attention in the least.

Something stabbed his heart and Nathanial caught his breath before coughing lightly so that his brother would not see it. Lady Amelia had come back to his mind, just at the very time he had told himself there was no young lady of interest within London. Why was *she* present in his mind? There could be nothing there for him to give attention to, surely? Lady Amelia had irritated him somewhat at the ball, given that she had a clear expectation for him to speak and converse with her during the ball while he himself had every desire simply to dance and remain silent. *And* she had the audacity to call him rude! Why ever would *she* be lingering in his thoughts? No doubt, Nathanial told himself as he rose from his chair, it was because she *had* been so very rude to him that he now found himself thinking of her.

"What is it that troubles you?"

"Troubles me?" Nathanial turned from where he now stood at the window, looking back at his brother. "Nothing weighs on me, brother. I was merely looking out and seeing what the day is like."

"The day is fine," came the reply. "Are you to join us for the fashionable hour?"

Nathanial's lips puckered. "The fashionable hour does not interest me."

"Why ever not?" William chuckled, clearly not in the least bit surprised at Nathanial's refusal. "It is an opportunity to see others and to *be* seen."

"And what if I have no wish to be seen?"

There came from William a heavy sigh which had Nathanial turning quickly. William had passed one hand over his eyes and was shaking his head and Nathanial's stomach tightened a little.

"What is it, brother?" His heart clattered in his chest. "Are you in pain? Is there something I can do for you?"

"I am not in any pain." William looked up at Nathanial again, his hand dropping to his side. "Brother, why are you in London?"

Nathanial blinked, his concern fading. "What do you mean?"

"Why are you in London?" came the question again. "Why did you come to London for the Season? It is not as though you have shown any real interest in being here, for while you danced a few dances last evening, you do not seem to be at all interested in the ladies you stepped out with. You have a disdain, almost, for the fashionable hour and for the thought of being seen by others. If

52

you are not in London to catch the attention of a young lady, if you have no desire to partake in society with any enjoyment, then why are you here? Would you not be happier back at your estate?"

For some moments, Nathanial could not find an answer. Instead, he looked away and folded his arms across his chest, his forehead puckering as he frowned. What was he to say to this? That when he had heard that Lady Amelia was to come to London and that their mother hoped to introduce William to her, Nathanial had found himself inexplicably drawn to the idea of coming to London? Even he himself could not truly understand why he had done such a thing as that! He had told himself he had been eager to see William – and that in itself was true – but there was also a desire to be where Lady Amelia was... mayhap to make sure that she did not speak of what had occurred between them the night they had met in the hallway.

"I – I wanted to spend time with my brother." It was the only answer he could give, an answer which his brother smiled at though there was still a flicker of uncertainty in his eyes.

"That is very good of you but you know I am to come back to the estate within a month or two. Could you truly not wait to see me?"

Nathanial closed his eyes and let out a slow breath. "I wished to come to London, that is all. There was no particular reason, though I *did* wish to be in your company again as I have said. After all, it has been some time since I have been in London – "

"Ah, there you both are!"

Nathanial was saved from having to make any further explanations by his mother who came sailing into the drawing room with some letters clutched in her hands. Her eyes were bright, her expression warm and she beamed at Nathanial as though he had done something quite wonderful.

"Good morning, Mother." Nathanial smiled briefly. "You appear to be rather... enthusiastic this morning."

"And why should I not be when we have received multiple invitations?" Lady Ashbourne exclaimed, waving the letters in Nathanial's direction. "It seems as though the *ton* is delighted at your presence, Ashbourne, as well as yours also." Turning to William, she beamed at him. "How glad I am to know that both of my sons have made such an impression upon the *ton*!"

53

"And my title has nothing whatsoever to do with that," Nathanial replied, wryly. "Mother, I am well aware of what society must be thinking about my presence here and that is the reason we have been invited to so many things."

Lady Ashbourne's smile faded a little. "I do not know what you mean."

Nathanial threw up his hands. "The *ton* think that, ah, the 'Beastly Duke' is in London, he must have come to find himself a bride! Though all of them have no intention of pushing their daughters to the fore nor their sisters either, for my reputation is so very dark that even those who do not care much for their children or siblings would consider doing such a thing as that! I am a spectacle, something to be viewed with suspicion and yet with morbid interest. My attendance at any such event will have more interest, more gossip and more whispers thereafter and thus, the hosts will garner a little more renown, will they not?"

Catching the way his brother frowned and waved one hand lightly in his direction, Nathanial came to a stop, seeing his mother's color fading slightly. Lady Ashbourne had closed her eyes and, her hand clenching into tight fists, drew in a long breath and lifted her chin just a little.

Then, she opened her eyes.

"You bring this reputation upon yourself, Ashbourne."

The stinging, sharpness of her words made Nathanial frown, his heart squeezing.

"You do *nothing* whatsoever to bring any sort of relief to this darkness," she continued, coming closer to him, one hand lifting, one finger pointing to his chest. "You seem to revel in it! I watched you last evening. I watched how you danced both with Lady Charlotte and Lady Amelia and how you passed very little conversation with either of them. There is no desire within you to be at all amiable! You are almost glad to have this dark reputation, are you not? You wrap it about your shoulders so that it clings to you and so that other people cannot come near you. Your brother is quite the opposite and the *ton* are glad to have him in society!"

Nathanial winced. "Mother, I would beg of you not to compare me to my brother."

"I have not endured what Ashbourne has done, Mother," William put in, though Lady Ashbourne immediately rounded on him, her eyes blazing with a sudden, furious fire.

"You have endured more! *You* were the one injured! *You* were the one near drowned and *you* are the one who continues to bear the consequences of that day and yet you do not behave as your brother does! You are amiable, smiling, laughing and conversing with those around you, relishing your life with every day that passes. Do not tell me that you have not endured in the same way as Ashbourne. You *have* endured, William albeit in a different way, but you have endured nonetheless! Instead of pursuing shadows and solitude, however, you have sought out brightness, good company and laughter. Society is delighted with your company but they turn an uncertain gaze to your brother." Looking back to Nathanial – who felt his heart squeezing painfully all the more – she shook her head at him. "You continue to choose this reputation, Ashbourne. Do not think I do not see it! It is a choice, day by day by day, to shield yourself behind these shadows and whispering dark. You claim to dislike the name 'the Beastly Duke' but I begin to believe that, in truth, you desire to keep it as close to you as can be. And I am heartbroken to see it."

Without giving him even a moment to respond, Nathanial's mother turned sharply and hurried to the door. Pulling it open, she rushed through it – but not before Nathanial heard what sounded like a choked sob breaking from her lips.

Chapter Nine

"Amelia?"

Looking up, Amelia smiled at her sister, her embroidery quickly forgotten. "Yes?"

"You – you have forgotten we were to go to Hyde Park for the fashionable hour?"

With a gasp, Amelia's hand flew to her mouth. "Oh, Charlotte! Forgive me! I was so lost in thought I quite forgot. Pray, indulge me but a few moments. I will change and be ready at the door. Call the carriage, will you?"

Charlotte smiled and caught Amelia's hand as she practically flew from the room, pulling her back. "Do not be too hasty. I have not found my bonnet or gloves as yet and Mama is still preparing herself!"

With a wry smile, Amelia hurried out of the room, up the staircase and to her room. Why had she forgotten about their plans to visit Hyde Park? They had already enjoyed some morning calls – though none of the gentlemen had caught her attention – and then, she had taken to her embroidery. Why had she forgotten about the fashionable hour?

"At least I am still wearing a suitable gown." Muttering to herself, Amelia went to the looking glass to make certain her face was quite clean and, thereafter, to choose which bonnet she was to wear. Her gown was simple but perfectly suitable, the shade a light green to match her eyes.

Which means I should wear a bonnet with a red ribbon. Picking it out, settled it on her head and made certain her curls sat in the right place, tying the ribbons and then finding herself wondering if the Duke of Ashbourne might be present that afternoon.

The thought made her stop short.

"Why ever am I thinking of him?" Murmuring aloud, she stared back at her reflection, taking in her wide eyes, the shock flickering in them as she blinked furiously, trying to understand what it was that she was thinking. Why would she care if the Duke of Ashbourne was present in Hyde Park? After their dance and his complete lack of interest in her company, she ought to be a little frustrated with him still, ought she not? She certainly should *not* be thinking about whether he'd be at the park and if she might catch his eye!

Closing her eyes, Amelia took in a steadying breath and then pushed those thoughts from her mind. Turning, she hurriedly picked up a pair of gloves and then made her way downstairs, ready to join her sister and her mother in the carriage.

***

"Good afternoon, Lord Wilcox." Amelia smiled at her new acquaintance, a gentleman she had been introduced to the previous evening, before dropping into a quick curtsy. "How very good to see you this afternoon. It is a fine day, is it not?"

The gentleman beamed at her, perhaps delighted that she recalled him. "It is a *very* fine day, Lady Amelia. You look to be in excellent health, I must say! The fresh air agrees with you, I think."

"Oh, but it does." Lady Stanton put one hand to Amelia's shoulder and sent a smile to Lord Wilcox. "My daughter is always out of doors, I must confess! Amelia loves nothing better than walking through the rose garden or making her way to the pond to see what fish are hiding there. My husband's estate is quite beautiful and very well managed."

"It sounds as though you have spent many happy hours there, Lady Amelia." Lord Wilcox spread out his hands, his head tilted a little in question. "Tell me, what is your favourite of all the flowers? I must know so that I might be able to offer you a bouquet, should the occasion arise."

A slight tendril of heat curled its way up Amelia's spine and she dropped her gaze for a moment. "I confess that, as my mother has said, I am very fond of roses."

Lord Wilcox nodded, still smiling. "Red, I presume?"

Amelia shook her head, catching his look of surprise. "I much prefer pink or even white or yellow," she told him, as his eyebrows lifted. "There are so many beautiful colours of roses and red seems much too popular for my liking."

"I shall remember that." Lord Wilcox smiled and then excused himself, leaving Amelia to turn to walk again with her mother, though she could not help but notice the smile which etched itself across Lady Stanton's face.

"You think him an interesting gentleman?" she asked, choosing to be direct rather than hide her questions away. "You think I ought to be willing to consider him, should he send a bouquet or come to take tea?"

"I think," Lady Stanton replied, reaching across to pat Amelia's arm, "that Lord Wilcox is something of a flirt. That does not mean that he is a gentleman who is not worth considering for flirtation and it does not mean that someone is unworthy of another but it is worth considering that a gentleman who is inclined towards flirtation and the like might not have any genuine interest in pursuing a true and genuine connection."

Amelia's shoulders dropped, her spirits dipping a little. "Oh."

"He was *very* charming," Lady Stanton continued, a light sigh escaping her. "But I do think that such gentlemen are aplenty and you would be wise *not* to consider them. Though you may very well receive a bouquet of yellow, white and pink roses from him very soon! He was a little too forward so soon after your first meeting and in that regard, I would ask you to be careful, my dear."

Amelia nodded. "I will." Glancing around the park, she took in the vast numbers of both gentlemen and ladies, seeing the carriages being driven slowly past. Silently, Amelia wondered if she might ever find herself a suitable match. Were the majority of gentlemen eager only for flirtation and teasing? Or were most of them eager to find a match?

"You need not worry, my dear." As though she had known what Amelia was thinking, Lady Stanton smiled at her. "There will be plenty of gentlemen coming to seek out your acquaintance and some will prove themselves to be more than perfect for you, I am sure. However, you need not make a match this Season, remember? Your sister is to be wed at the end of the Season and thereafter, you might consider your own future – but that could be in the Season still to come. At this time, let yourself be contented with making new connections and permitting the *ton* to know who you are. Though," she continued, with a light smile, "if you should find a gentleman who captures your attention in a way no-one else ever has done or ever will then of course, you *must* permit yourself to consider him!"

Amelia smiled back at her mother, seeing the twinkle in her eye. "I can assure you, Mama, there is no-one who has caught my attention as yet." As she spoke, the twinge in her heart reminded her of the Duke of Ashbourne but she ignored that without too much difficulty.

"Ah, but you have not even been in London for a fortnight!" her mother exclaimed, a teasing smile still on her lips. "Though I will still advise you against Lord Wilcox, no matter how charming he seems to be!"

Laughing, Amelia leaned into her mother. "I will, though I will be appreciative of any flowers he wishes to send me!"

"Might I have a word with you, Lady Amelia?"

Catching her breath with surprise, Amelia turned just as the looming figure of the Duke of Ashbourne stepped beside her. Lady Stanton stopped quickly, turning Amelia towards him though she herself managed to put a smile to her face.

"Your Grace, good afternoon." Amelia bobbed a quick curtsy, aware of just how quickly her heart was pounding. "You wish to speak with me?"

"Yes, if you please." Looking to her mother, the Duke gave a brief smile though it did not touch his eyes. "It will only be a few minutes, Lady Stanton, and I will return her to your company just as soon as the conversation is at an end. We will stand just here, if you will permit it."

Lady Stanton cleared her throat gently, clearly a little uncertain though she looked to Amelia as though she was the one who ought to answer. Amelia blinked rapidly, her surprise still rattling through her heart as she then glanced again at the Duke.

"If my daughter is willing to stand and speak with you, then yes, I will permit it," came the eventual reply. "Though I must ask, Your Grace, is it something of importance that you wish to speak to my daughter about?"

Again came that brief smile but again, there was no flicker of light in his eyes and Amelia's stomach dropped.

"It is an apology I wish to make, Lady Standon," he told her, though he did not so much as glance at Amelia as he said this. "That is all."

"An apology?" Lady Stanton looked to Amelia but she could only lift one shoulder before letting it fall again, having very little idea as to what it was that the Duke meant to apologise for. "Then of course, Your Grace. Please, take as long as you need." With a lingering glance in Amelia's direction, she gave her a small nod and then stepped away though only a very short distance.

Amelia looked up at the Duke expectantly, taking in the way his dark hair fell across his forehead, though he brushed it back carefully as if aware of her scrutiny. Lifting her eyebrows, she waited for him to speak, trying to ignore the way her heart pounded furiously.

"Thank you, Lady Amelia." The Duke coughed though kept his gaze away from her, and the way he shifted from one foot to another, his hands clasped behind his back, made her believe that he was a little uncertain or unsure, perhaps even of himself. "As I have said to your mother, I have come here to make an apology."

"Yes, I heard." Amelia lifted her chin a notch. "What is it you wish to apologise for, Your Grace? From what I can see, there is no injury here."

"Ah, but what you said of me last evening at the ball was quite true," came the quick reply as, finally, his blue eyes settled on hers. "You spoke to me of my lack of conversation, stating that I was being somewhat rude in my unwillingness to converse. I will admit to you now, Lady Amelia, that having considered your words, I see them now to be quite true. I beg your forgiveness."

Amelia could not prevent her mouth from dropping open such was her surprise. The Duke of Ashbourne was apologizing to her? And what was more, apologizing for something she had thrown at him? It was certainly not at all what she had expected.

"Goodness, I must truly be something of a beast if that is your reaction." The muttered response of the Duke to her evident shock made Amelia's heart flutter with mortification, heat pouring into her cheeks as she quickly shook her head.

"No, of course not, Your Grace, you are no beast. Though I will admit to being rather surprised at your apology."

His eyes sought hers. "And for what reason would that be, if it is not that I am not a bit of a fiend?"

Amelia forced a smile, aware of how her blood was thrumming wildly in her veins. "It is a shock that any gentleman should listen to a lady they have only danced with on one occasion and who spoke with such sharpness to them," she replied, aware of the heat in her face. "And I will confess to being sharp in my words and in my tone, Your Grace. Forgive me in that."

Much to her surprise, the Duke quickly shook his head. "No, Lady Amelia, not in the least. There is no guilt upon you, no apology that you need to make. I was the one who acted poorly. I should have been willing to set aside my own preferences and make the dance all the more enjoyable for you. I should have spoken to you, I should have responded to your questions with more eagerness rather than by dismissal."

Amelia nodded. "Yes, you should have, Your Grace," she responded, with alacrity. "You stated that you find no purpose, no enjoyment in answering questions in that regard though might I offer another perspective?"

The Duke nodded slowly. "You may."

"You might find yourself enjoying the dance all the more, should you begin to engage in conversation," Amelia stated, seeing his eyebrows lift. "That is to suggest, however, that you enjoy the dance even a little in the first place!" When his eyebrows dropped and he pulled his gaze away, Amelia could not help but laugh – albeit rather ruefully. "You do not care for dancing either, then?"

"I had not danced in a long time, prior to last evening." The Duke pushed one hand through his hair, a long hiss of breath escaping him. "It is not that I do not enjoy such things, Lady Amelia, it is only that I am not used to them."

Amelia tilted her head, considering. The Duke of Ashbourne appeared to be speaking with nothing short of honesty and she appreciated that, she supposed. "You have not often been in society?"

"No." He lifted his shoulders. "I have not had any desire to be so."

"But you are in London now."

"Yes, I am. Though I carry something of a dark reputation which, I am aware, I continually seem to spread through society given my disposition." He rubbed at his chin. "I *am* the Beastly Duke."

Spreading out her hands, Amelia smiled, an idea coming to her. "Then, if you wish to find yourself a little happier in society, would you not let me help you?"

The Duke's eyes grew wide, his hand falling back to his side. "What do you mean?"

"Permit me to help you," she repeated, though the idea – now that she thought of it a little more fully – was, no doubt, immediately going to be dismissed by the Duke. "If you wish it, at any social occasion we happen to be at together, then I might, perhaps, be present with you, aiding in conversation and the like so that you do not appear so severe."

The Duke's lips quirked and Amelia immediately dropped her head, mortification searing through her. He *was* going to laugh at her, mock her suggestion and tell her that the last thing he needed was her help.

"Pray, forget that I ever made such a suggestion. I – "

The Duke's hand caught hers just as she turned away. Sparks shot up her arm and she spun back towards him, only for the Duke's *other* hand to reach out to steady her. The smile on his lips faded away, his eyes rounding as he looked at her. Amelia swallowed hard, looking back at him as he released her, though his gaze remained steady.

"I was not about to laugh at you, Lady Amelia. Your suggestion is nothing but kindness itself." Putting one hand to his heart, he inclined his head. "If you think that you can do anything to encourage my reputation to be a little less than darkness, then I should be glad of it."

Amelia's eyes rounded, surprise pushing through her heart. "Truly?"

"I mean every word," he swore, the severity of his gaze convincing her. "I do not know what it is you can do but – "

"I might have to correct you at some points," she interrupted, seeing him frown. "I already admitted that I spoke harshly to you last evening at the ball given that I thought you rude. What happens if I must do so again? Will you turn from me? Will you give me a curt answer and thereafter, turn away entirely?"

The Duke cleared his throat, considering. Looking away, he took in a breath and then, nodding to himself, returned his gaze to her. "If you wish to speak to me in such a way, if I am deserving of such firmness, then yes, I shall accept it. My mother and my brother have both spoken to me this very day of my reputation and of my seeming desire to cling to the 'beastliness' spoken of me. I wish to prove them wrong. I wish to prove to myself that I can do a good deal more than simply remain within my own house and linger in my own company."

Again, surprised by his honesty, it took Amelia a few minutes to regain her speech. Seeing that there was no lie in his eyes, no teasing smile at the edge of his mouth, she let out a slow breath and then nodded. "Very well. We have an accord, Your Grace."

A flitting smile lifted his features and on seeing it, Amelia's breath hitched, her eyes flaring as heat rippled from the top of her head all the way down to her toes.

"It seems that we do, Lady Amelia."

"Might I ask if you are to be at the ball this evening? Lord and Lady Jeffersons' ball?"

He nodded. "I am."

She managed a smile, despite the fact that every part of her seemed to be suddenly all of a tremble. "Then let us see if this evening might bring any sort of improvement to your reputation, Your Grace."

The smile on his face grew and Amelia averted her eyes for fear that the heat within her might grow all the more. It was not often that she had seen the Duke of Ashbourne smile – even less, seeing him smile with a genuine happiness in his eyes – and now that it was there, now that it was ever present, lifting his features, she did not quite know what to do with the feelings that such a small thing brought to her. Much to her relief, her mother came to stand by her elbow, inquiring whether they were now quite contented, given the smile she had seen on the Duke's face. Amelia heard the Duke of Ashbourne's retort, confirming that indeed he had articulated everything he deemed necessary and that Amelia had been most kind in her understanding, and then he took his leave.

"That seems to have gone very well. I do not think I have ever seen the Duke smile in such a way."

Hearing the note of interest in her mother's voice, Amelia looked to her at once. "He apologised for being very brief in his conversation during our dance last evening, that is all."

"That was very good of him."

Amelia laughed, chasing away the strange sensations within her heart. "I would have preferred it from him last evening so that the dance might have been a little more enjoyable, but I shall accept his apology nonetheless."

"That is good." Lady Stanton took her arm and then they began to walk together. "We should go to find your father and Charlotte now, for we cannot linger long. There is still dinner and then the ball this evening!" She looked to Amelia. "Are you looking forward to it?"

"I – I am." Amelia frowned, a little surprised at just how much she was looking forward to stepping into Lord Jefferson's house and into his fine ballroom. But was it the ball she was so excited about? Or was it the company she was to find within?

Chapter Ten

"Mother?"

Nathanial inclined his head as his mother turned towards him. "You look quite radiant, I must say."

His mother smiled. "Thank you, Ashbourne. You are very kind."

"No, I am not." Seeing how her smile immediately disappeared, Nathanial sighed and shook his head. "You spoke to me with great directness this morning, Mother. I want you to know that I have been considering what you said."

A faint hint of color climbed into her cheeks. "My son, I spoke harshly. I did not mean – "

"You were quite right to do so." Taking his mother's hand, he pressed it gently as an unfamiliar sensation – though not unwelcome – began to wind through him. "I am sorry. I *have* been clinging to this shade, this name which the *ton* have spoken of me. You are quite right in that regard. I have thought my own company to be the very best of company. I have thought to stay away from society because I simply did not wish to go amongst them. I have clung to my regret and my sorrow over what happened to my brother, what *I* did to my brother, for many a year."

"But you have no need to cling to it."

Hearing his brother's voice, Nathanial turned sharply, seeing William walking towards him, his limp barely noticeable now.

"I have told you such a thing already and still, you are determined to linger in this." William stopped by them both, his eyebrows lifting. "Why are you so determined?"

Nathanial shook his head. "It does not matter why. What matters now is that, having listened to both of you, I have decided to set aside the mantle which I have long carried. Indeed, my initial thought was that I would return to my estate very soon upon my arrival in London but now, I have set upon staying a little longer."

Lady Ashbourne pressed his fingers back in return. "That is good, Ashbourne. You should learn how to move about society again. And society needs to see that you are not what they think you are."

"Alas, I think they may be wrong in that regard." Nathanial offered his mother a wry smile. "I have been beastly in my dark demeanour, in my unwillingness to join society and to reject all kind invitations and the like. However, I have looked at my life and my behaviour and have chosen to alter myself, where I can."

Both his mother's and William's eyes rounded at once and Nathanial's stomach twisted sharply. Was that truly coming to him as such a surprise?

"I already apologised to Lady Amelia for the blunt manner with which I spoke to her last evening," he continued, dropping his gaze to the floor. "And I will continue to apologise if I must, to whomever I injure or upset in my manner as I learn what it is to be a better, happier fellow."

A short silence met his words and Nathanial glanced from one to the other, suddenly a little concerned that what he had said would be either laughed at or ignored, as though he would not be able to do such a thing. Instead, his brother gave him a friendly tap on the shoulder and when he looked into his mother's eyes he saw that Lady Ashbourne was blinking rapidly as though she were pushing her tears away.

"That is wonderful to hear, my son." Her voice grew hoarse and she squeezed his fingers again. "Come now, let us make our way to the ball." With a breath, she smiled at him, her eyes still a little glassy. "How thrilled I am to hear it, Nathanial. Truly."

It was not often that his mother called him by his Christian name and Nathanial felt the weight of it settle on his heart. When she turned to walk to the carriage, William following after her, Nathanial paused for a moment, aware of the tension clawing through his stomach. Yes, he had determined to change his ways and yes, he had Lady Amelia's very kind offer to guide him through such things but all the same, a strange tension lingered within him.

He could only pray that this evening would yield some profitable results.

***

"Good evening, Lady Katherine, Lady Goodfellow." Nathanial inclined his head, seeing how mother and daughter exchanged a glance. "I do hope that you are enjoying your time in London?"

66

Again, there came another quick glance though it was Lady Goodfellow who spoke rather than her daughter. "Yes, Your Grace. How very good of you to ask." She offered him a quick smile and then looked to her daughter, her eyes rounding as she urged her silently and yet clearly enough, to speak to the Duke thereafter.

"It has been very pleasant."

Lady Katherine's voice was more like a squeak, her gaze darting all over the place as she sought to find a place to settle her eyes. Evidently, she was a little uncertain about looking at him directly and Nathanial frowned, only then to pull that from his features, realizing it would make him appear displeased.

"And have you been to many balls?" Trying to find something to say, something to ask to a young lady who appeared to be more than a little terrified of speaking to him was very difficult indeed. Nathanial attempted to keep his expression as banal as he could, struggling to offer her a smile given the frustrating way she began to stammer and stutter, making the conversation all the more difficult.

"Thi...this is... this is my... my... "

"Ah, good evening, Lady Katherine, Lady Goodfellow. How very good to see you both. I am sure you both remember my sister, Lady Charlotte?"

Nathanial let out a slow breath, relief filling him as he looked into Lady Amelia's eyes for a moment, only to catch the way that Lady Katherine let out a great rush of breath, clearly more than a little relieved that her conversation with him had been so interrupted.

"Good evening, Lady Charlotte, Lady Amelia." Lady Goodfellow smiled and then gestured to Nathanial, though her smile flickered a little. "We were just speaking to the Duke of Ashbourne, who was asking Katherine if she had been attending many balls of late."

Lady Amelia smiled warmly at the young lady. "This is only my second ball, Lady Katherine. Have you been to more than I?"

"Yes, though not too many. This is my seventh ball of the Season and they are all more than a little enjoyable! Indeed, I find it very difficult to say which one I enjoyed the most!"

"I am sure that will continue, the more balls you attend," Nathanial interjected, catching the uncertainty flickering in Lady

Katherine's eyes as she glanced at him. "I intend to throw a ball this Season also, though it is not something I have ever done before. Tell me, ladies, if you might, what does one need to make a very successful and, as you have said Lady Katherine, an enjoyable ball?" It was not a question he truly needed answered for, to his mind, the answer was more than obvious. All that was required for a successful ball was a superb orchestra, food and drink provided for the guests and a ballroom that was beautifully decorated – and with gardens open to the guests also, should it be possible. What else was there for him?

"I think the first thing that is required, Your Grace, is to have those of good character invited to your ball."

Nathanial's shoulders slumped immediately. This was not at all what he had thought of. "Good character?"

Lady Katherine bit her lip and looked away but Lady Amelia was instantly ready to encourage her.

"What would you say to that, Lady Katherine? Recall that His Grace has been absent from society for some time so whatever explanation we can give him will be of great benefit, I am sure." Lady Amelia glanced to him and Nathanial quickly nodded, looking again to Lady Katherine who, thankfully, had stopped biting her lip.

"Yes, that is just so, Lady Katherine. Might I ask you to explain a little more about what such a term means?"

Lady Katherine glanced to Lady Amelia and then, after a moment, continued. "I mean to say that there must not be those who are rogues or scoundrels at your ball for to have them present means that a lady must constantly be on her guard. It does not bring a great deal of enjoyment to have to continually be watching for those who would be unwelcome company."

Nathanial frowned, one hand rubbing at his chin. "And would such gentlemen truly seek out the company of young ladies?"

"Yes, of course they would!" Lady Amelia laughed rather ruefully as a tiny hint of a smile touched Lady Katherine's lips. "A rogue certainly enjoys going to seek out which young ladies he might be able to convince to stand up with him. So I would quite agree with Lady Katherine, if your guest list does not include such fellows, then that is an excellent idea."

"And you should not have any prolific gossips either," Lady Katherine put in, now warming to the subject. "Not that I like to speak ill but there are those within the *ton* who enjoy coming to events and occasions so that they might thereafter whisper about it, spreading rumours about this person or that. I would be careful in your invitations in that regard also, Your Grace."

Nathanial swallowed hard, the idea of throwing a ball now battling hard against his mind for, having thought it would be a particularly easy occasion to organize, he was now beginning to fear that there was a good deal more to it than he had first thought. "I see."

"Then, of course, there is the orchestra," Lady Katherine continued, as Lady Amelia nodded. "There must also be no watered wine, if you wish to have a good report thereafter."

"Watered wine?" Nathanial frowned. "I know that there were some who add water to their wine when the guests are to be thirsty but – "

"Oh, it is not because they think the guests will be thirsty but rather because they believe it is a way to make certain they do not have a particular expense." Lady Amelia smiled, tilting her head a little as she looked up at him. "You are unaware of such a thing, mayhap? You have not been in society for some time."

A ripple of heat ran across Nathanial's chest and he coughed, spreading out his hands. "It seems as though there is a good deal I do not know or understand, Lady Amelia. I am grateful to you both for your suggestions. I will think of everything you have said and use it when I am to go ahead with my ball."

Lady Katherine smiled warmly and Nathanial let out a slow, surreptitious breath, relieved that she was smiling at him still, at the very least. This appeared to be a genuine smile, he considered, and was certainly a good deal better than when he had first attempted conversation with her.

I have Lady Amelia to thank for that.

"I look forward to this ball, whenever it should take place," Lady Amelia said quietly, as Lady Katherine nodded eagerly, a slight flush in her cheeks now. "Thank you for asking us for our opinion, Your Gracee. It is not often that such a thing occurs."

"Indeed, it is not!" Lady Katherine exclaimed, as though she had only just thought of such a thing. "Thank you, Your Grace."

"We look forward to your ball." Lady Goodfellow, who had been standing to one side so that they might all converse without her interjection, came back to fetch her daughter from Nathanial's side. "Thank you for your conversation, Your Grace. We are both very appreciative."

Nathanial inclined his head and watched as Lady Goodfellow led her daughter away, leaving him to stand by Lady Amelia who was, he noted, smiling broadly. Evidently, she was rather pleased with what she had managed to achieve in turning the circumstances from a tight, tense situation to a flowing conversation. Lady Charlotte had turned to another young lady near them and was in deep conversation, leaving him alone to talk to Lady Amelia openly.

"Thank you, Lady Amelia." With a gruffness to his voice that he had not intended to be there, Nathanial glanced at her and then looked away. "You came to my aid, it seems."

"I did." Lady Amelia's smile grew as he looked away, clearing his throat. "I was glad to do so. You see now that Lady Katherine took her leave of your company without believing that you are 'beastly' as she might have thought at the beginning?"

"I do." Admitting it aloud was not as difficult as he had feared and, to his surprise, a broad smile began to spread across his face. "Perhaps this partnership will be more than a little successful after all."

Chapter Eleven

Abby brushed Amelia's red curls in long, gentle strokes as Amelia herself let out a slow breath of contentment, finding herself smiling as she recalled what had happened last evening at the ball. She had not seen the Duke of Ashbourne today but there was to be a soiree tomorrow which, she had learned, he would be attending.

"What is it that makes you look so happy?" Abby tilted her head as Amelia looked at her maid in the mirror's reflection. "I must say, your delightful smile has been consistent ever since you took a seat here!"

Amelia smiled and then lifted her shoulders. "The Beastly Duke and I have come to an accord."

"The Beastly Duke?" Abby's face grew a little concerned. "You are not in company with him, are you? I have heard a lot of things about him and none of them have been good."

"I am." Amelia lifted her shoulders a little and then let them fall. "You are right that there are a lot of rumours and whispers about him and I will admit that a good many of them are true for he *is* dark in his manner and his demeanour is less than pleasing. However, I have discovered that he has more to his character than what is supposed. Recall when Charlotte and I went to his estate to visit his mother?"

Abby nodded, her eyes a little rounded with evident surprise at Amelia's description of the Duke of Ashbourne. "Yes, I recall that night. I was worried about you in the storm and then there came word of your decision to reside at the Duke's estate overnight."

Amelia smiled. "That night, I stepped out in the early morning because I had heard something. The Duke was in a state of distress and I learned from him that his dreams had been tormenting him. Apparently, it is something that has happened often and though he begged me to keep what had happened to myself – which I promised to do, of course, for I am not inclined to adding to rumours – I saw more of his character and, perhaps, the reason for some of his shadowy moods."

"You still must be careful. The Duke of Ashbourne seems, to me, to be a gentleman of an unsettled nature."

"He did not tell me what it was in his dreams that terrified him, as he himself said." Amelia let out a small sigh, her shoulders dropping a little more. "But I saw a man broken by fear and that made me deeply sorry for him." Her eyes lifted again to her maid. "You must promise me not to tell anyone what I have told you. Not even the other maids."

"Of course I won't." Abby's gaze was steady and Amelia looked back at her carefully before nodding. Abby's many years of service and loyalty to Amelia made her absolutely certain that she could be trusted and Amelia appreciated that.

"What is this accord you've come to with him?" A slight flush touched the maid's cheeks. "If it's alright for me to be asking."

Amelia's smile returned. "I will be helping the Duke of Ashbourne to make a better impression upon society."

Abby frowned. "What do you mean?"

"To help the *ton* to think better of him rather than continue to believe that he is 'beastly'," Amelia explained. "We had our first attempt at this yesterday evening at the ball and it went very well. What had been a staid and difficult conversation with Lady Katherine turned into a very enjoyable conversation for us all, I think. Lady Katherine left our company with a smile rather than the worry I saw in her eyes when I first joined them."

"That is very good of you, Lady Amelia." Abby finished brushing Amelia's hair and then set the brush down. "Why did you offer such a kindness?"

Amelia opened her mouth to respond, only to frown. "I – I do not know. Perhaps it is because of what I witnessed the night I was present in his manor house, or because of what he said to me when he apologised for ignoring me during our dance. Either way, I have decided that I will do my best to be of aid to him."

"Even though you are meant to be enjoying your own Season?" The maid's eyes twinkled. "What if the Duke of Ashbourne becomes more of a consideration for you than your own standing within society?"

"He will not." Seeing the spark in her maid's eyes, Amelia understood what her maid was asking and quickly flung it aside. Yes, she would admit that there was an interest in the Duke of Ashbourne but she had already realized just how different they were in terms of character. While she was glad and contented to be of aid to him, she could not let her feelings grow to anything significant. The last thing she required would be to have the Duke of Ashbourne settling in her heart, for while his dark demeanor was lifting just a little at present, there could surely be no contentment between a gentleman with such a heavy weight upon him and herself. He did not strike her as the sort of gentleman who would enjoy walking through the rose gardens or enjoying an evening stroll! No, he was a gentleman who sought out his own company, preferred solitude to company and would lose himself in books rather than in beautiful gardens. As she prepared herself for bed, Amelia continued to reflect on the differences between them and became slowly more and more convinced that the Duke of Ashbourne could never be anything more to her than he was at present.

***

"Good afternoon, Lady Charlotte. Lady Amelia."

Amelia smiled and inclined her head. "Good afternoon, Lady Blithe. Good afternoon to you also, Lady Violet."

Lady Violet was known to them both from previous encounters and she smiled warmly, though Charlotte was the one who drew closer and began to speak more at length with her. They were closer in age and subsequently, a little closer in acquaintance. Lady Blithe began to speak to Amelia's own mother and Amelia herself was left standing between two lots of chattering ladies and had nothing else to do but remain silent.

A glance over her shoulder and she spied a bookshop. Though it was somewhere which often caught her interest, on this occasion, she found herself quite eager to go inside. It would give her mother and sister ample opportunity to converse with their friends while she perused some books for something more to read.

"Charlotte," she murmured, catching her sister's arm for a moment. "Tell Mama that I am gone to the bookshop, should she require me. I will only be a few minutes."

"Oh, we will join you!" Lady Violet exclaimed as Charlotte nodded. "Let me just tell my mother where we are to go."

After a moment, Charlotte, Lady Violet and Amelia turned to walk the few steps into the bookshop. The day was very fine indeed and most of the *ton*, Amelia considered, would be either in Hyde Park or St James' Park so they might see or be seen by many a society member. Not many would be in a bookshop! Pushing the door open, she stepped inside and smiled at the man at the counter, who gave them all a nod but said nothing more. There was a silence here in this shop, a quietness which made Amelia's spirits lift as she made her way around the shelves of books, taking in each and every one. Even the chatter between Lady Violet and Charlotte softened and Amelia turned around to glance at them, smiling gently at how they had both stopped to look at one particular book together. Turning back around, Amelia continued to wander to the very end of the bookshop, the books now becoming a little dusty as though the bookshop owner had decided that no-one would want to look at these particular books and thus, had neglected them a little. For whatever reason, these books intrigued her, wondering what it was about them that made them so neglected. Running her fingers along the top of one, she clicked her tongue lightly at the amount of dust which now clung to her finger.

"Lady Amelia."

A low, dark voice made her jump, her skin prickling as a figure stepped out from the gloom. Not quite recognizing him straight away, she stared back at the figure, only for his voice to reach her again.

"I did not know you read."

"Your Grace," Amelia stammered, her heart pounding furiously. "Good afternoon. I – I am here with my sister and Lady Violet. I – "

"I should not have startled you, forgive me." The Duke inclined his head and then smiled briefly, though his eyes remained a little shadowed. "I did not think that you were someone who enjoyed a great deal of reading."

Amelia lifted an eyebrow, irritation pushing away her surprise. "Your Grace, you do not know me at all. How could you say such a thing as that?"

The Duke opened his mouth to respond and then closed it again, though a slight flicker entered his eyes. "Yes, you are quite right." He ducked his head. "I ought not to have said such a thing.

Tell me, Lady Amelia, do you like to read? It is something that you enjoy?"

"I do, as it happens. Though I do not often read," she admitted. "I embroider during the day for it is something that I can do as well as converse, for there is always someone to talk to!"

The Duke smiled at this. "That is understandable." Clearing his throat, he looked past her to the door. "I should take my leave. I – "

"Are you not going to permit me time to speak with you?" Amelia took a small sidestep, coming to stand directly in front of him. "After all, it would be a little rude for a gentleman to ask the *lady* some questions, only to then step away when his questions are at an end, without giving her any opportunity whatsoever to ask him questions of her own!"

The Duke of Ashbourne paused, then looked back at her. "I suppose I could be persuaded to linger in conversation for a little longer." The edges of his lips lifted. "Is there something you would like to ask?"

"Yes." A few questions came to her mind – questions about what he had been dreaming about the night she had discovered him in the hallway, questions about why his dark moods continued to linger so, but Amelia chose to push all of them to one side. Instead, she asked only a simple question, aware that they did not know each other particularly well as yet. "Might I inquire as to whether you like to read, Your Grace?"

His smile did not return. "Yes." There was a heaviness to that word, a weight which seemed to sink him down and bring their conversation low. "I have often enjoyed reading. Though it is a singularly solitary activity, is it not?"

"Which you often indulge in."

"I do." Wincing, he shook his head. "Though I am attempting to indulge in it a little less."

"Because you wish to gain society's favour a little more."

His shoulders lifted. "Mayhap. I am not certain what it is that I desire, Lady Amelia. All I know is that I do not want to be known as 'the Beastly Duke' any longer. Though it seems as though I do require your help in that regard."

Amelia found herself stepping forward, her hand going to his arm as sympathy rippled through her chest. There was a sadness to his tone, a frustration in his eyes which did not seem to fade even though her hand settled on his. Instead, his shoulders appeared a little slumped, his lips pulling into a flat line.

"You will achieve that, Your Grace, I am sure of it."

His eyes closed. "And yet even here, even in London in the company of my brother and in other fine company, I find that my dreams still linger. They still grow and spread and put out dark fingers over my soul."

At the mention of his dreams, Amelia pressed her fingers on his a little more. "What can be done to rid you of these, Your Grace? It is clear that they torment you and yet – "

"Nothing can be done." The Duke looked down sharply as though he had only just realized that her hand was on his and then, pulling it away, stepped back. "Forgive me. I should not have said anything." A scowl pulled at his features. "It seems as though I cannot make even a single moment of considerate, respectable conversation without either frightening the young lady I am speaking to – such as Lady Katherine – or expressing something I ought not to have done. I think I shall take my leave of you now, Lady Amelia, before I say anything more foolish."

Amelia wanted to tell him to stay, wanted to tell him that there was nothing wrong with what he had expressed and that she would be glad to listen to whatever it was he wanted to say but the Duke of Ashbourne had already walked away before she had time to truly think about what she might say to encourage him to linger. With a heavy heart, she turned and watched him walk not only away from her but right out of the bookshop, letting the door close behind him without so much as a single glance in her direction. Swallowing hard, Amelia was a little surprised at the upset which filled her heart and soul, the sadness which came with the realization that her attempt to be of aid to the Duke could only go so far. If he had no desire to express the truth to her, had no eagerness to share with her what he struggled with, what brought him so much sorrow, then what else could she do? Yes, she might aid him in conversation and speak well of him to others but if he could not express the singular difficulty, the one thing which continually tortured his mind and entered into his dreams, then what hope was there for any real, significant change in his heart and his character?

Tears began to sting in her eyes but Amelia blinked them away furiously, refusing to let them fall. She was *not* about to let herself become so caught up with the Duke of Ashbourne that she let her heart grow heavy and sorrowful over him. With a sniff, she lifted her chin and returned her attention to the books, doing everything she could to push the gentleman out of her mind.

Chapter Twelve

Nathanial looked up as his mother came through the door of the drawing room. "Mother. You look quite lovely. Are you ready to attend the soiree?"

"I am." Lady Ashbourne began to smile, only for that to fade as she walked over to him and then placed one hand lightly against his cheek, her eyes searching his. "You are troubled."

Nathanial, who had not been able to remove the most recent conversation he had shared with Lady Amelia from his mind, instantly shook his head. "I am quite well, Mother, I assure you."

"I do not believe you."

A quiet laugh broke from Nathanial's lips. "Be that as it may, Mother, I assure you that I am not troubled. I – "

"You have not been sleeping." Lady Ashbourne tilted her head, her hand dropping back to her side. "I have heard you wandering the hallways at all hours of the night. I do not sleep well myself and often rise to read so do not pretend to me that you have been without difficulty. I know that not to be true."

Letting out a slow breath, Nathanial shook his head. "What else can I say, Mother? I am better than I would be if I were at home, I am sure."

"I doubt that." There was a hint of mirth in Lady Ashbourne's voice and though Nathanial frowned, he saw her smile. "You would be more than contented back at the estate, I think. You would be enjoying the quiet, the solitude, the peace that you so often crave. Instead, however, you have given yourself to a different situation entirely where you are forced, now, to be in company and to do the very opposite of what you usually enjoy."

Nathanial could not help but chuckle, seeing the truth in his mother's words. "I will not pretend otherwise."

"But all the same, I think it is good for you to be doing this," his mother told him, just as William came into the room. "Though I do wonder if there is a young lady who has caught your interest?"

"Ashbourne? Find himself drawn to a young lady?" William laughed as he came towards them both. "Come now, Mother! We must be reasonable in our expectations and not suggest things that are quite out of the ordinary for this Duke." Clapping one hand on

Nathanial's shoulder, he grinned broadly at him. "Is that not right, brother? You are here only to attempt to rejoin society a little, nothing more."

Nathanial nodded. "That is just so. I am afraid I have no interest in any young lady, Mother, though do not think I have forgotten my responsibilities in that regard. At some juncture, I will begin to consider matrimony but it is not at the present moment."

"I see."

"Though perhaps I shall," William put in, making his mother beam as Nathanial's eyebrow lifted. "I have met many a pretty young lady, though I must admit that Lady Amelia seems to me to be quite lovely. Her sister is too and I should have looked to her first but given that she is already engaged, I cannot – and will not – do so."

A stone dropped into Nathanial's stomach.

"Lady Amelia is perfectly lovely!" Lady Ashbourne exclaimed, slipping her arm into William's as they turned to make their way from the room and down to the waiting carriage. "And the daughter of a Marquess, so she is already more than suitable for you."

William chuckled. "I would not let someone's title – or lack thereof – prevent me from pursuing someone, should I truly wish it," he told his mother as Nathanial remained rooted to the spot. "Though I will let myself consider Lady Amelia, certainly. Her beauty, her gentle manner and her delightful conversation make her a diamond in my eyes."

The door closed and Nathanial stared at it, his breathing a little shallow as he tried to take in what his brother had said. There was no reason for him to be feeling so astonished, he told himself, but a light sweat had broken out across his forehead and heat was burning flames up his spine.

William? Considering Lady Amelia? Squeezing his eyes closed, Nathanial let out a long, slow breath as he fought to make sense of what his brother had said. There was no reason why William should not consider Lady Amelia, given that she was both a debutante and more than amiable, so why then was he himself finding that thought so troubling? He had known from the beginning that his mother had hoped to introduce William to Lady

Amelia but Nathanial had never once thought that William would truly consider her!

I must say something.

The moment that thought came to him, he snatched it up and threw it away. What was it that he thought he could say to his brother? He could not tell him to stay away from Lady Amelia, could not suggest that he should look to someone else, not without William asking him for an explanation – and what then would he say?

With a groan, Nathanial forced himself to walk forward, walk to the door and down towards the waiting carriage. He did not want to have to attend this soiree any longer, he realized, pulling out his handkerchief to dab at his forehead. He did not want to be in any place where his brother would be in prolonged conversation with Lady Amelia... and where he would have to witness it.

***

Scowling, Nathanial kept himself to the back of the library, watching the other gentlemen and ladies as they sat to play at cards. He had entered the house, greeted their hosts and had then stepped away from everyone, including his mother and his brother, choosing to retreat into solitude rather than watch the moment his brother found Lady Amelia and sought out her company.

"Your Grace!" A young lady beckoned to him, her eyes alight with interest. "Might you wish to join us?"

Nathanial's scowl remained, noting how Lady Katherine sat next to this particular young lady. No doubt Lady Katherine had shared with this young lady – whoever she was – that Nathanial was not as much of a beast as was said and therefore, this young lady was reaching out to him in the hope of his company.

"I do not think we have been introduced." Clearing his throat, Nathanial lifted his chin, seeing the smile on the lady's face begin to fade. "Forgive me, I do not think I can join you."

The young lady blinked. "We... we have been introduced, Your Grace. Else I would not have asked you to join us. I am not at all improper."

Nathanial heart twisted and he cleared his throat, recognizing that he had not only embarrassed the lady but was in such a dark mood that to continue on in this vein would only bring him more difficulty. One single remark by his brother had been enough to push him back into a dark state, he recognized, and that was not acceptable. Besides which, it was not fair on this young lady who had been bold enough to reach out to him.

Nathanial coughed and then stepped forward, attempting to smile though it did not spread easily across his face. "You must forgive me for forgetting our introduction. There have been many new acquaintances and though I am a Duke and used to meeting a great number of people, it is still rather difficult to remember everyone. Might you remind me of your name?"

The young lady glanced to Lady Katherine, worry now shining in her eyes. "I should not have called out to you, Your Grace," she replied, not doing as he had asked and Nathanial silently cursed his own foolishness in acting as he had done. "Forgive me."

"There is nothing to forgive," he replied, growing suddenly desperate to make amends to this young lady. No doubt he had also given Lady Katherine a worse impression of him. Lady Amelia's good work was already being broken down – and he was the one doing it. "Please, do remind me, if you would."

"You have not forgotten the name of an acquaintance, have you?"

A light, bright voice broke through Nathanial's desperation and he looked directly into the twinkling eyes of Lady Amelia, seeing her give him a tiny nod, obviously aware of what was going on. "Goodness, that is quite unforgiveable, Your Grace!"

The teasing manner in which she said this had both Lady Katherine and her companion glancing at each other, though a tiny smile began to touch the edge of the lips of one.

"I am afraid I have. As I have explained, I have met so many new acquaintances of late that not all of them linger in my mind."

"Which I suppose, is a reasonable excuse." Lady Amelia laughed and shook her head at him, before turning her attention back to the two ladies. "You shall have to forgive him, I think. After all, the Duke of Ashbourne has not been in London very often these last few years and as such, is unused to being required to recall a good many names, such as we are!"

The second young lady glanced again to Lady Katherine before finally, looking back at Nathanial. There was a hint of a smile there and her expression was certainly less concerned than before .

Once again, Nathanial recognized, he was in debt to Lady Amelia.

"I think I shall forgive you, Your Grace," the lady said, making Nathanial let out a breath of relief as he bowed his head to express his thanks. "I am Lady Violet. My father is the Earl of Blithe."

"Of course." Were he to be truthful, Nathanial would tell the young lady that alas, he still did not recall being introduced but he chose not to say such a thing. He had upset her enough already. "What is it you asked of me, Lady Violet? It is to play cards?"

As Lady Violet nodded, Nathanial glanced to Lady Amelia, seeing her smile and then immediately step away. His hand reached out of its own accord but he quickly pulled it back. He could not ask her to linger, could not ask her to stay, not when she had done exactly as she had said she would do and had helped him, once again, to have a better standing in society. How remarkable was that, with only a few words, she had managed to repair what he had managed to shatter.

"Will you sit with us, Your Grace? Even if you will not play, you might advise me for I am quite sure that I have forgotten exactly how to play!"

"As have I!" Lady Katherine added, her cheeks a little pink. "I am sure we will both require your help."

Nathanial forced a smile and nodded, taking the seat proffered. The truth was, inwardly, he had absolutely no desire to be sitting beside Lady Violet and advising her on what card to play or what the rules were. Instead, he wanted only to be in company with Lady Amelia, finding her so very different to him that it was as though she were the only solution to his darkness. Turning his head, he glanced to where she was standing, only to see his brother step forward and, inclining his head, smiling at Lady Amelia as she bobbed a quick curtsy towards him. Nathanial's stomach cramped and he turned his head away, pulling his gaze in the opposite direction from his brother and Lady Amelia. All the same, however, he found his thoughts tugging towards them, unable to concentrate on the cards being dealt.

"I have it!"

Getting to his feet, Nathanial forced a quick smile as he looked to his brother again. "I think it would be just the thing to have my brother join us. What say you, Lady Katherine, Lady Violet? After all, it would be rather difficult for me to advise you both, would it not? What if my brother, the Marquess of Highcroft, came to join us? He might sit with one of you and I might sit with the other. That way, you will both be given the aid you require."

The two ladies glanced at each other but, much to Nathanial's relief, nodded with eagerness in their expressions. A thrill of relief ran up Nathanial's spine as he strode across the room to his brother, seeing how William's gaze ran to his.

"Highcroft," Nathanial began, once Lady Amelia had finished speaking. "Might I be so rude as to steal you away?"

"Steal me away?" William frowned. "I am just now speaking with – "

"I have two young ladies eager for help when it comes to playing cards," Nathanial interrupted, aware that he sounded much too happy about this though he hoped Lady Amelia and his brother would not be able to understand why. "I cannot help them both at the same time. Might you come to sit with us? That way, you might be able to aid Lady Violet and I might aid Lady Katherine – or the other way around. I do not mind. I simply cannot help two ladies at once!"

William blinked but it was Lady Amelia who spoke next, encouraging William to do as Nathanial had asked.

"But of course you must go! Lady Violet is a dear friend of my sister's and I know she would be glad to have the company of either of you fine gentlemen."

With a small smile, William inclined his head. "I do hope we will be able to continue our conversation together at another time?"

"But of course."

Nathanial smiled, a sense of triumph washing over him. "Thank you for being so gracious, Lady Amelia. Come, Highcroft. They are waiting." With a nod to Lady Amelia, Nathanial turned back to the waiting Lady Katherine and Lady Violet, his brother falling into step beside him. For the moment, at least, he had salvaged the situation and that was a small victory, at least.

Chapter Thirteen

Amelia looked back at the Duke of Ashbourne, watching him as he smiled at Miss Jennings. The last sennight, she had seen the Duke of Ashbourne do rather well, though she had needed to step in on more than a few occasions. Lady Violet had spoken with Charlotte at length as to how rude the Duke had been when they had first asked him to join them for cards at the soiree last week, though Amelia had been glad that the first impression had been somewhat improved thereafter.

A slight pang of what felt like jealousy broke through her heart and Amelia quickly turned her head away. She was not about to let herself feel anything for a gentleman so different to her and who, she reminded herself, showed no particular interest in her either. She was aiding him in his attempts to better his reputation in society and he was doing that very thing by greeting and conversing with as many young ladies as would give him opportunity. The fact that he was a Duke, of course, did not make that particularly difficult though there were still plenty of whispers about him. He was rather brooding still, certainly inclined towards dark moods and the rumors about him having a beastly character were still ongoing. Society was slow to change its opinion on anyone, Amelia considered, though she was glad, at least, that he had begun to improve a little upon them.

And he has improved a great deal upon me.

"Good afternoon, Lady Amelia! I see that you too have decided to take the air this fine afternoon."

Amelia turned and then smiled warmly at Lord Highcroft. "Yes, Lord Highcroft, I have. My mother and sister are just there, talking to Lady Hawkridge, though I myself was in conversation with Lady Sarah although she has just taken her leave."

"Then permit me to take her place, if you would?"

Amelia nodded and smiled, though noted the flash of interest in Lord Highcroft's eyes. Her stomach tightened, suddenly a little concerned that Lord Highcroft might have more than a little interest in her company. As yet, she had not truly considered him – had not considered any gentleman of note – but that did not mean, she reminded herself, that they had not thought of her.

"Tell me about your estate, if you would," she said, hoping that it might encourage him to give her a long explanation so she might then begin to think about how she could make certain that Lord Highcroft's interest did *not* linger on her. There must be someone else he might consider!

"I have only settled there the last year," Lord Highcroft began to explain. "It is not too far from my brother's estate, perhaps a day and a half's travel. Once I finished at Eton, I decided to take on the Grand Adventure and went around the world to explore what I could! I did not tell my mother, however, for fear that she would be deeply upset and worried for me so instead, I simply wrote when I could and said very little of what I was doing!"

"I see." Amelia smiled at him, thinking that there was a tension between truthfulness and consideration in what he had done. "Do you like your estate, Lord Highcroft? I must confess that I adore my father's house. The gardens especially are beautiful."

"With yellow and pink roses, yes?"

Another voice came over her shoulder and Amelia glanced towards it, frowning as none other than Lord Wilcox ambled towards them. "Yes, that is so, Lord Wilcox."

"I have not forgotten, you see." Tapping his nose, Lord Wilcox grinned at her, ignoring Lord Highcroft entirely. "How very fine a day it is to be out of doors. Mayhap you would like to take a short stroll with me, Lady Amelia?"

Amelia bristled. "I should not." She gestured to Lord Highcroft. "As you can see, I am in conversation with Lord Highcroft. In addition, my mother and my sister are standing just over there and – "

"You are a cripple, are you not?"

The sharp, rude manner of Lord Wilcox had Amelia catching her breath, her eyes widening with utter astonishment at Lord Wilcox's rudeness. She had never once dreamed of mentioning Lord Highcroft's small limp – a limp that was barely noticeable most of the time – and yet Lord Wilcox thought it perfectly acceptable to say such a thing? She could hardly believe it.

"Lord Wilcox, I – "

"I do hope that your manner is not the same when you converse with young ladies as it is when you speak to other gentlemen, Lord Wilcox." Lord Highcroft arched an eyebrow

86

though his tone grew rather firm. "That is a very pertinent question and not one that I would expect from a gentleman such as yourself."

"Then you do not know me very well," came the reply, as Lord Wilcox grinned in a way that had Amelia's skin prickling. "I have observed you, Lord Highcroft, and have noticed your difficulty. Why do you not speak of it? It is not as though you can hide it."

"Because it is my business what I speak of and to whom I speak of it." Lord Highcroft lifted his chin. "And I certainly would have no desire to speak with you, Lord Wilcox, I can assure you."

"I am sure it is only wise to be open about such things." Lord Wilcox sniffed and threw one hand out towards Amelia. "After all, young ladies such as Lady Amelia, the daughter of a Marquess, should be fully aware of the sort of gentleman they are speaking with, the difficulties that such a gentleman has so that they do not get too closely acquainted with someone who can never fulfill the sort of requirements that a young lady – such as Lady Amelia – expect."

Amelia drew herself up, quite certain that her face was scarlet with anger and upset. "I do not think that I require *your* comments and remarks in that regard, Lord Wilcox," she stated, her hands clenching into tight fists so that she might outwardly keep her composure. "And I can assure you that I would much prefer to spend time in the company of a gentleman such as Lord Highcroft than be in the company of a gentleman who does not know how to speak with kindness, compassion or consideration."

Lord Wilcox frowned as if, somehow, what she had said displeased him, as though she were deliberately being foolish in her response. What else had he expected? Had he thought that she would join him in his questions? That she would turn on Lord Highcroft and demand answers about the injury to his leg? The gentleman was incredibly imprudent if that was the case!

"Do you truly think that it is acceptable for a gentleman such as yourself to be speaking to another in that way?" she continued, as Lord Wilcox' lip curled. "I hardly think you are displaying any sort of gentlemanly behaviour by doing so, Lord Wilcox. Rather, I think, you display your own lack of finesse and consideration for your fellow man!"

"You are the daughter of a Marquess, Lady Amelia," came the quick reply. "You ought to be very careful in your consideration of which gentlemen – and ladies also – you decide to keep company with. My remarks came from a desire to express that concern to you for mayhap you were unaware of Lord Highcroft's limp for he is very good at disguising it."

The more Lord Wilcox said, the angrier Amelia became. She wanted to rail at him, to demand that he should fall silent rather than say another word about the matter, but instead, her anger grew so great that *she* was the one who could say nothing. All she could do was shake her head.

"Yes, Lord Wilcox, I have a limp." Lord Highcroft spoke quietly though when Amelia looked to him, she saw the fire in his eyes and the fury in the way he tightened his jaw. "It happened when I was child. However, I have *never* had it affect my character in any way. A physical ailment does not make one's character any less."

Amelia nodded. "As you yourself display, Lord Wilcox. You have no physical ailment, it seems, but yet your character is a good deal more questionable than that of Lord Highcroft. In fact, Lord Highcroft, I do not think that I have any interest in conversing with Lord Wilcox any longer." Turning her head away from Lord Wilcox, who had, by now, began to scowl darkly, she looked to Lord Highcroft. "Mayhap you might accompany me back to my mother?" They were only a short distance away and Amelia could easily have walked there alone but she spoke in the hope that Lord Highcroft would be willing to walk with her so they might step away directly from Lord Wilcox. Thankfully, Lord Highcroft seemed to understand and simply offered her his arm and, without another word to Lord Wilcox, stepped away from him at once.

"I am truly sorry for what Lord Wilcox said," Amelia murmured, as Lord Highcroft took her closer to her mother. "That must have been upsetting."

Lord Highcroft managed a small smile. "It is not as though he is the first gentleman to notice that I have a limp," he said, quietly. "He is the first, however, to speak of it in such a blunt manner!" He laughed a little ruefully. "Though there is nothing for you to apologise for, Lady Amelia. It is not as though it was your doing."

"It is only because I am acquainted with him that he spoke with us," Amelia murmured, her face still hot as her anger slowly faded away. "Though I shall be doing my utmost to stay away from him now, I think."

"No-one would blame you for that." Lord Highcroft smiled. "And I believe I shall do the same, Lady Amelia."

It was at this juncture that her mother turned to look at them both and Amelia was forced to bring an end to their conversation. Lord Highcroft and her mother spoke together for a few minutes and thereafter, Lord Highcroft took his leave. Amelia let out a slow breath as he walked away, though her gaze went to a gentleman standing a little further away, his head turned in their direction as though he had been watching them both and was interested in everything that had taken place.

The Duke of Ashbourne.

Amelia's breath caught in her chest, her whole body tightening as she gazed back at him, unable to pull her eyes away from his. She did not know what it was he was thinking, did not know why it was that he was watching her with such interest but all she could do was simply hold his gaze. In watching him, she quite forgot about Lord Wilcox, forgot about what had happened between Lord Highcroft and him, forgot about her anger and upset. All she could do was look into the Duke's face and, as she did so, found herself desperately hoping that he might come over to speak with her.

He did not.

Instead, as his brother approached him, the Duke finally pulled his gaze away from Amelia and began to speak with him instead. Amelia did not have to wonder what it was they spoke of for such a darkness came into the Duke's expression that she knew Lord Highcroft was telling his brother about Lord Wilcox. With a sigh, she turned her head away, seeing her mother looking at her with obvious concern in her eyes.

"I am quite well, Mama," she said, quickly. "It is only that Lord Wilcox spoke so very rudely to Lord Highcroft that I find myself upset over what was said. The gentleman is not kind, I must say."

Her mother shook her head. "I did tell you that Lord Wilcox was something of a flirt, did I not? It seems as though he does not have a good heart either. You would be best to stay away from him, I think."

"Yes, I believe so." Amelia glanced again at Lord Highcroft but the Duke of Ashbourne and he were already walking away. "I do hope Lord Highcroft was not too injured by what Lord Wilcox said... and that nothing more comes of it."

Chapter Fourteen

Nathanial scowled. "I think it ridiculous that a gentleman such as Lord Wilcox would *dare* say such a thing in front of you – or in front of anyone, for that matter!"

"He is not a pleasant fellow, I think." William shrugged his shoulders. "What else is there to be said? Someone we do not need to keep company with, certainly."

"I would agree." Nathanial ran one hand over his face and let out a slow breath, aware of the tight knot inside him. His dreams about William and their childhood accident continued to burn, his evenings still not as calm and as pleasant as he might like. The Season had continued to go well, however, and with Lady Amelia's help, he was doing a little better in terms of how those in society viewed him. This, however, only added to his current frustrations and his lingering guilt about his brother. If he had not been as foolish at the time, if he had stayed close to his brother and had not permitted him to fall into the pond, then William would not be facing the ridicule and the remarks now.

"You need not look so frustrated." William sat back in his chair and let out a slow breath, sighing contentedly as he stretched out his feet in front of him, crossing them at the ankle. "It is not as though it troubles me."

"Does it not?" Looking around Whites, Nathanial took in the other gentlemen present, noting how none of them were looking in his direction. No doubt his reputation preceded him but for the moment, Nathanial was contented just to being company with his brother. "It troubles me, I will admit."

"It should not." William lifted his shoulders and then let them fall, reaching up one hand to catch the attention of the footman so he might order them both something to drink. "IT is not as though there is anyone else who is concerned with my limp. And Lady Amelia who was with me at the time set Lord Wilcox in his place."

"Lady Amelia?"

William nodded, quickly giving the footman his order before returning his attention back to Nathanial. "Yes, she was with me. Did you not see me with her?"

"I saw you standing with her mother."

"Ah, that was only when we had walked away from Lord Wilcox. I returned her to her mother and then came to speak with you."

"Though you did not tell me everything he had said until this moment."

Again, his brother shrugged as though this was of very little consequence. "What does it matter?"

"I – I would have said something to him."

"Which is, mayhap, precisely why I did not tell you." A quirk pulled at William's lips. "You would have stormed over to him, no doubt, and ruined what you are currently building in how society views you."

Nathanial scowled. "That matters not."

"Yes, it does." Accepting the glass of brandy from the footman, William gestured for the man to give the other one to Nathanial. "I know what you have been doing in your attempts to have society no longer think of you as 'the beastly Duke' and in that regard, I can see that you have been making some progress which is an excellent thing, I must say. I would not want you to do anything to ruin that. Not when it has taken you so much effort."

Nathanial snorted, a hint of a smile at the corner of his mouth. "Do you truly think it has taken me so much energy?"

"I do not *think* it has, I *know* it has," his brother countered, chuckling. "You are a man who is entirely inclined to his own company. You do not like to have the company of others. You are not desirous of conversation and the like. Rather, you would prefer to sit alone in your study and read as much as you wish, without interruption. Is that not so?"

Something stirred in Nathanial's heart. Something unsettling and uncomfortable and taking a sip of his brandy, he let the liquid burn gently down his throat before he answered. "I do not know if that is the truth, brother," he said, slowly. "I have always been inclined to my own company, that much is true, but whether it is because I truly wish for such a thing or because I have simply become that way due to my own choices, I cannot say. It is not something that I wish to continue on with, however and now that I consider these last few weeks, though I am still eager for my own company at times, I can say truthfully that I am finding a little more enjoyment in what is being offered to me here."

William's eyebrows lifted. "Is that so?"

"Yes, it is." Nathanial took in a breath and then smiled. "Though I should mention that a good deal of that is thanks to Lady Amelia." Seeing the curiosity on his brother's face, Nathanial chose to be truthful. "She offered to aid me where she could, offered to come and speak to those near me or to interject where required so that I would not appear as dark and brooding as I truly am! She has been able to help many a young lady continue on a conversation with me and has, on more than one occasion, saved me from my own foolishness."

"Goodness." William's astonishment brightened his features. "I had no knowledge of this. I must say, this improves my consideration of the lady all the more!"

"As it should," Nathanial admitted, aware of the twinge in his heart over his brother's interest in Lady Amelia. "Lady Amelia is the very spirit of generosity. There is a kindness about her which I have never seen in anyone else. Without her, I am sure that I would have ruined myself here in London already. Society would have called me the 'dreadful, beastly Duke' or some such thing, and I would have returned to my estate without any thought of returning."

His brother smiled gently. "Then I am glad that you have stayed," he said, quietly. "I do think this is good for you, brother, though you might not be particularly pleased to hear me say such a thing. I have seen our mother's happiness in this also, as I am sure you have."

"I have." Nathanial let out a slow breath, letting himself relax just a little. "Perhaps you are right. I would, no doubt, have done something foolish had you told me the truth at the time. I – " His gaze caught on another gentleman as he entered the room and in an instant, his frustrations soared all over again, anger beginning to bubble in the pit of his stomach. "And now, it seems, fate has decided that the very gentleman we are speaking of is to appear."

William frowned and then turned, just as Lord Wilcox strode a little further into the room, his chin lifted and his gaze roving around the room as though he were deciding which person was best suited to his company. His gaze settled on Nathanial and then shifted to William, only for a smirk to catch the edge of his lips. Turning on his heel, he walked to the opposite side of the room... and Nathanial's ire roared to life.

"Be still." His brother reached out, setting one hand on Nathanial's chair. "I can see that you are already irritated by Lord Wilcox's presence but you must not permit yourself to be so. We are going to be in company with him very often, I am sure. Why then should we permit ourselves to be frustrated by his company?"

"Because when he speaks evil it ought to be called out for what it is," Nathanial replied, darkly. "I will not have people speaking ill of you."

"Yes, you will." William chuckled, surprising Nathanial with his reaction. "You cannot always protect me, brother, though you are kind to think that you must do such a thing."

Nathanial frowned. Was that what he thought? What he believed, deep down? Was he of the mind that he ought to somehow save his brother, even though they were both full grown men?

"I appreciate your desire to quieten Lord Wilcox, truly," William continued, though his tone was quieter now. "But the best thing to do in this situation is to remain silent and ignore him. Let him speak his insults. The only person who gains darkness and the society's chagrin will be him."

In his heart, Nathanial knew that this was so but all the same, his irritation grew as Lord Wilcox looked over at them again. Picking up his brandy, he threw it back again only to then slam the glass down hard on the table, frustrated beyond measure that he could not seem to find a way to remove his anger from himself. "Perhaps I shall take my leave. Mayhap – "

"Did you know that I sent Lady Amelia a very large, very colorful bouquet of roses?"

Lord Wilcox's voice was loud enough for Nathanial to hear and with the sharp look which the man sent to him, he was certain that it was meant to be heard by both William and him.

"I said something which upset her, though I do not think that I said anything wrong," Lord Wilcox continued, laughing harshly as he spoke. "It was done just to please the lady, which I am sure you can all understand."

This sent a ripple of laughter around the room though Nathanial looked away, his jaw tightening as he fought the urge to rise to his feet and stride out of Whites. He did not need the *ton* to become aware that there was any difficulty between Lord Wilcox and himself. No doubt there would be questions as to where it came from and, Lord Wilcox being the sort of gentleman he was, would, no doubt, use it as an opportunity to make himself appear quite excellent and without fault while adding to Nathanial's 'beastly' reputation.

"Lady Amelia was defending Lord Highcroft!" Lord Wilcox exclaimed, throwing one hand out towards William. "Can you imagine it, gentlemen? A young lady coming to the aid of a *gentleman*?"

Nathanial's jaw tightened all the more and even William shifted in his chair, frustration settling across his face, his eyes narrowing though he kept his gaze away from Lord Wilcox.

"A Marquess need not be defended by a *lady*," Lord Wilcox laughed, as the mirth in the room rose all the more. "It was quite ridiculous, I must say. What a fool you must feel, Lord Highcroft!"

"I do not feel at all foolish," William replied, turning in his chair and looking directly at Lord Wilcox though he did not rise from his chair. Nathanial noticed that his brother's hands were white, gripping the arms of the chair as he spoke as he too felt the very same anger spiraling within him. "Lady Amelia is free to say whatever she wishes. I would not prevent her from speaking her mind."

Lord Wilcox chortled. "Of course you would not. But, then again, you are not the sort of gentleman to have any strength of character... given that you have a lack of strength in your frame. I suppose the two go alongside each other, do they not?"

Nathanial was out of his chair in a moment as the room fell entirely silent. Anger was pouring through his veins, burning through him as he strode right across the room. Lord Wilcox rose to his feet just as Nathanial reached him but Nathanial did not hesitate. Grasping the man by the lapels, he hauled him closer, hearing the gasps from the other gentlemen watching.

He did not care.

"Are you attempting to speak ill of my brother, Lord Wilcox?" he asked, his voice booming across the room. "Are you attempting to slight him, to make fun of the limp he has, just as you did during your conversation with Lady Amelia?"

Lord Wilcox's eyes rounded and Nathanial shook him, hard. He was a full head taller than this gentleman and was willing to use both his height and his strength to his advantage.

"Well?" he exclaimed, seeing the way Lord Wilcox's eyes rounded with obvious fright. "Did you mock my brother for his injury? Is that not why Lady Amelia attempted to speak against your harshness, so that my brother's limp would not become as much of a focus as *you* were attempting to make it?"

"Ashbourne." A hand on Nathanial's shoulder told him that William was beside him now, encouraging him to release Lord Wilcox. "There is no need."

"There is *every* need." Releasing Lord Wilcox just a little, Nathanial kept his fingers wrapped around the man's lapels. "Should you *dare* speak of my brother again in this manner, should you even utter one word in the same vein as what you have already said, then I *will* call you out, Wilcox. It will be pistols at dawn for the insult you have laid upon my family."

Eventually releasing him, he watched as Lord Wilcox staggered back, one hand going to his throat as though Nathanial had choked him. It was only then that he realized just how heavily he was breathing, how fast his heart was going and as his brother dropped his hand from his shoulder, Nathanial came to see that every eye was now on him. There was nothing but utter silence now, the last words he had spoken hovering on the air.

Heat burned from his toes to the very top of his head.

"You... you seek to threaten me?" Lord Wilcox squeaked, his eyes bulging out of his head. "You lay so many claims at my feet stating that I have said this or said that and yet you give me no opportunity to defend myself!"

"There is nothing that you can say by which to defend yourself."

It was not Nathanial who spoke now but William himself, his voice rising as the obvious anger in his eyes ran down into his voice.

"You stated to me directly, in front of Lady Amelia, that I was a cripple."

A gasp ran around the room and Lord Wilcox dropped his hand from his throat, his eyes roving around after it, as though he understood now that he was not about to be exonerated by his own words.

"You, thereafter, stated that ladies such as Lady Amelia ought to be aware that gentlemen such as myself, because of my physical difficulty, could never fulfill the requirements that a lady of her standing would expect. Quite how you thought it acceptable to say such a thing – not only to myself but also to Lady Amelia – is quite beyond me. I gave you opportunity to apologise but you only insisted that you were doing so out of concern, though I do not think that even Lady Amelia believed that given how eager she was to step away from you!"

Another gasp ran around the room and Lord Wilcox wilted, his shoulders dropping. "I – I did speak out of concern," he stammered, now seeming to be a little flustered. "But I did not mean to be – "

"We all heard you speak this evening," Nathanial interrupted before Lord Wilcox could pretend to be truly apologetic. He had no doubt that the man would somehow try to make out that still, William or Nathanial – or them both – were the ones who had caused trouble. "It is as I have said, Lord Wilcox. Say another word about my family or my brother where your words hold a sting, hold an insult, then it will be pistols at dawn."

Lord Wilcox's eyes flashed and Nathanial's lip curled. This gentleman was precisely as Nathanial had expected, a snake hiding his true nature from them all.

"It is a strong reaction, Your Grace," Lord Wilcox stated, speaking slowly so that everyone in the room could hear what was said. "Though I suppose that is what should be expected from 'the Beastly Duke'."

Nathanial's lip curled, fire igniting in his heart and he took a step forward, just as a murmur rang around the room as the gentlemen watching them whispered about what Lord Wilcox had said. "That is something I would consider to be an insult, Lord Wilcox."

"Would you?" Any supposed sorrow and regret in Lord Wilcox's voice and expression faded. "Everyone in society knows you as such. It is not as though I am saying anything out of the ordinary." His eyebrow lifted, a glint in his eye. "Are you to call out everyone who calls you such a thing, whether you know it or not?"

Growling, Nathanial took another step forward, one finger pointed to Lord Wilcox's chest. "Do not start questioning me, Wilcox. You have done enough already. Heed my words. I will *not* pull back from what I have stated."

Without another word, Nathanial turned on his heel and made from the room, sure that his brother was following after him. His hands clenched tight, his ire growing still but as he made his way out, he was certain he heard Lord Wilcox's voice following after him.

"He truly is the Beastly Duke."

Chapter Fifteen

"Did you hear what happened?"

Amelia looked to Lady Violet, hearing the tone of her voice and wondering at the seriousness there. "Hear about what?"

"About what took place between the Duke of Ashbourne and Lord Wilcox? It is quite shocking!"

Amelia shared a look with Charlotte who was also frowning, perhaps uncertain as to whether or not they ought to indulge in what neither of them liked to hear. They did not want to take part in spreading gossip and rumor but, all the same, if there was something about the Duke of Ashbourne that had taken place, she certainly did want to know of it.

"When did this happen?" Charlotte asked, as Lady Violet looked over her shoulder, perhaps concerned that someone else was walking nearby in St James' Park and would overhear them. "Recently?"

"Only two days ago," Lady Violet replied, her voice a little quieter now even though no one was nearby. "Lord Wilcox evidently insulted Lord Highcroft, calling him a cripple and other such things, which I think is quite awful!"

"I can confirm that he did do such a thing," Amelia interjected, seeing Lady Violet's eyes widen. "Evidently it has not reached the ears of society but I was standing with Lord Highcroft when Lord Wilcox said such things to him. It was shocking and I made my displeasure quite clear, I can assure you."

Lady Violet blinked. "Goodness, how awful." Her lips pulled into a soft smile. "I think Lord Highcroft is an excellent gentleman, I must say. I do not even notice the slight limp and he is certainly not a cripple!" Her eyes flashed suddenly. "And even if he were, that would not take away from his character!"

Amelia nodded in agreement, noting the interest that she both heard and saw in Lady Violet's voice and expression. Could it be that she had a quiet affection for Lord Highcroft?

"Well, apparently the Duke of Ashbourne took very badly to this insult and the day after, in Whites, he strode across the room, grabbed Lord Wilcox by the throat and offered terrible threats should he dare say a word about Lord Highcroft again!"

Amelia closed her eyes briefly, a sigh tugging up through her chest. "I see." She knew in that one moment, everything that the Duke and she had built by way of improving his reputation upon society had crumbled into dust. It was not as though she believed that everything which Lady Violet told them had happened just as she had said, but even the rumors were enough to damage him irrefutably.

"I am sure that the Duke of Ashbourne had every right to defend his brother *and* his family name." Charlotte sent a sympathetic look toward Amelia, perhaps realising the frustration which now rushed through her. "It may not be as bad as you have heard, Lady Violet."

"Oh, undoubtedly it is not exactly what took place," Lady Violet agreed, quickly, "but all the same, *something* took place."

"Something that does not put the Duke of Ashbourne in a particularly favorable light," Amelia sighed, rubbing a line at her forehead. "I am sorry to hear it."

"It may be that the *ton* think it understandable that the Duke of Ashbourne should have behaved so," Lady Violet suggested. "After all, hearing that Lord Wilcox said something so very dreadful about Lord Highcroft is greatly shocking."

Amelia nodded slowly but despite Lady Violet's reassurances, felt herself sink slowly into a melancholy. She had begun getting to know the Duke of Ashbourne a good deal better and she certainly could not imagine him grabbing Lord Wilcox by the throat in such a dark manner! Even though he was still heavy in his expression, his character had changed a great deal these last few weeks. Could it be that there was this genuine anger, this explosive frustration which could bring Lord Wilcox to injury? She shuddered lightly, despite the warmth of the sun. *Mayhap there is a side to the Duke of Ashbourne's character that I do not know. Mayhap he can be violent.*

"No."

Both Charlotte and Lady Violet looked to her at once and Amelia flushed, her face hot. "Forgive me, I was thinking aloud."

Charlotte smiled. "You were thinking that the Duke of Ashbourne could not possibly have grasped Lord Wilcox around the throat in the way that Lady Violet has described – not that I think you speak ill, my dear friend, but only that what has been told to you is not the full truth."

"I was, yes." Amelia let out a small sigh. "Though I am sure that he came to the defence of his brother. After what I heard Lord Wilcox say to Lord Highcroft, even *I* was ready to strike him!"

"It is awful," Lady Violet murmured, quietly. "Lord Highcroft does not deserve such things spoken about him."

"No, he does not." Amelia smiled at her friend. "I shall speak to him directly, I think. I – "

"There is your opportunity."

Amelia came to a sudden stop as, coming around the path just ahead of them, came the Duke of Ashbourne, walking beside his brother. Both of their expressions were grave, their heads close together as they spoke. Amelia's stomach flipped over and she caught her breath as the Duke's eyes caught hers, only for him to come to an immediate stop.

"Lady Amelia." Coming forward quickly, the Duke inclined his head. "I am very glad to see you. I should... forgive me." Clearing his throat, he smiled at Lady Violet and then to Charlotte. "Good afternoon to you both."

"Good afternoon," they echoed, though Amelia looked to Lord Highcroft rather than to the Duke.

"Lord Highcroft, I believe that Lady Violet would very much like to express her concern over what Lord Wilcox said of you of late." Seeing the surprise jump into both Lord Highcroft and the Duke's expression, she spread her hands. "The rumours are already spreading across London, I am afraid, though Lord Wilcox does not come off particularly well."

Lady Violet immediately began to speak to Lord Highcroft, her words quick and her voice passionate, while the Duke of Ashbourne reached out and caught Amelia's hand – though only for a moment – and just long enough to catch her attention.

"I was to write to you." He heaved a sigh and ran one hand over his eyes. "I had hoped that it would not be spread through society but my mother heard something this morning and fear now that I am to be let down in my hope."

"I believe so." Amelia looked up at him, searching his face. "Did you grab Lord Wilcox by the throat and attempt to choke him?"

The shock on the Duke's face was so stark, Amelia was embarrassed to have even suggested it.

"My dear lady, I did no such thing!" The Duke's face grew red, his voice a little more fervent as he came a fraction closer to her. "I would not strike a man simply because I did not much like him or because he had spoken an insult or two against my family."

Amelia put out one hand to his arm. "Forgive me, I ought not to have asked such a thing. I should have known that you would not have done so. In truth, I did doubt it though that is, I am afraid, the rumours which are currently spreading through London."

The Duke's eyes went to where her hand rested on his, only to then pull up to her face as she dropped her gaze. "I am sorry that there are such rumours. That is not what I did, though I will admit to grabbing the man by his lapels and warning him to keep his insults away from William *and* from myself. I warned him that if he continued, then I would have no other choice but to call him out."

Amelia did not much like the idea of the Duke and Lord Highcroft standing with their pistols, ready to shoot at Lord Wilcox and he at them but, all the same, she could understand his desire to protect his family's name and reputation. "I see." Her shoulders lifted and then fell. "Though that is not the same as grabbing someone by the throat and throwing threats to him."

"No, it is not. I did not threaten him either, I only stated that there would be consequences if he continued to speak about my family in that particular manner. That, I think, is perfectly reasonable."

"After what he said of Lord Highcroft – even directly to him – I can understand that," Amelia replied, a little ruefully. "The gentleman seemed to take great pleasure in saying whatever he could to insult Lord Highcroft, though I could not understand why. He stated that he did so for my sake, though I think that utterly preposterous."

"As do I," came the reply, though the Duke did not smile. "Thank you for understanding the situation, Lady Amelia. I am grateful for it."

"Though," she responded, quickly, "the *ton* will not understand as well as I do, Your Grace." Her lips twisted for a moment. "I – I fear that they will find you now more 'beastly' than

102

ever, even though you did not do anything wrong, it seems. Lord Wilcox will do whatever he can to make the situation appear best to his advantage, I am sure. The *ton* will not look at you the same way." A small sigh escaped her and she looked away. "It seems that our attempts to improve your reputation and to remove the 'beastly' term from you may now have come to an end."

"I am sorry about that but – "

"I do not think that you need to apologise." An idea suddenly came to Amelia and she caught her breath, looking up suddenly, wide eyed, at the Duke of Ashbourne. He waited, clearly aware that she wanted to say something and looking at her quietly rather than asking her what was in her thoughts. The idea swirled this way and that, letting her thoughts run from one place to the next but the more she considered it, the more it seemed to be an excellent thought.

"I – I have just thought of something. I do not know if it would be of any good or if you yourself would even *consider...* " Closing her eyes, she took in a deep breath. "I am being too hasty." Opening them again, she saw the Duke smiling at her and the softness in his expression sent her heart turning over in her chest. There was almost a tenderness there, a gentleness which she could not fully understand.

"Why do you care so much about me?" The Duke's question made Amelia's eyebrows lift in surprise, realizing that she had no immediate answer to give him.

The Duke tipped his head just a little, his gaze now a little more intense. "Why is it that you wish to come to my aid in such a way, Lady Amelia? No one else cares as much as you seem to do. After all, this was my doing and the *ton*'s response to my actions – or the rumours about my actions – will be just as they decide. It is not for you to concern yourself with, Lady Amelia, and yet that is precisely what you are doing."

Amelia swallowed at the tightness in her throat, searching her mind for a reason that she felt so passionately about coming to the aid of the Duke of Ashbourne and yet realizing that she could not express the truth to him, a truth that she was only just realizing herself.

She cared for the Duke of Ashbourne.

Yes, she had been trying to keep her feelings away from him, had attempted to keep her heart as cold and as closed to him as she could and yet, as she looked up into his eyes, there was nothing she could do to prevent her heart from leaping towards his.

"Perhaps it is because I know that you are not 'the Beastly Duke', as they call you," she said, her voice tight and a little rasping. "I do not like the unfairness of it all."

"But again, that need not concern you," the Duke replied as Amelia dropped her gaze to the ground. "However, that is not my focus here, I suppose. I should be grateful – and I *am* grateful – to you for your willingness to come alongside me, even though I do not feel as though I deserve it."

Amelia pressed her lips tight together so she would not respond without thinking, her heart pounding a little more quickly as she searched her heart and came up with the very same response. Her main reason for aiding the Duke of Ashbourne was because she was now beginning to care for him – and care for him in a way that made her heart leap with both fright and joy in equal measure.

"Mayhap I will tell you about this idea of mine, mayhap I will not need to." Heat ran down her spine as she managed to smile back into his eyes. "The *ton* may forget about this, they may not even remember about it for something else might come to take its place on the rumour mill."

The Duke chuckled. "Mayhap. I can be hopeful, I suppose."

Amelia nodded. "Of course. Are you to attend the ball at Almacks this evening?"

"I am. My brother and my mother are to attend also."

Amelia smiled. "Then I look forward to seeing you there, Your Grace."

That softness came back to his eyes as he inclined his head, his voice holding a gentleness which had not been there before. "As do I, Lady Amelia."

Chapter Sixteen

Walking into the ballroom, Nathanial felt his skin begin to prickle as what felt like a thousand eyes all turned to look at him at the very same time. He had expected the *ton* to notice his arrival, certainly, but he had not expected this amount of study. It was almost as though everyone was watching him, expecting him to do or say something that would validate everything that they thought about him given the rumors which were now spreading through society about him.

He sighed and kept his head lifted, his shoulders dropping as he looked around at the many faces turned to his, noting how their gazes slipped away as their eyes met his. Obviously, those in the *ton* were embarrassed to be seen watching him but no doubt, many of them would be more than willing to *speak* about him behind his back, as though that were perfectly acceptable.

"I shall defend you to everyone I speak to," his mother murmured as Nathanial offered her a small smile in thanks for her kindness. "I know that you did not do what is being said."

"I did not throw Lord Wilcox against a wall and attempt to choke him, no," Nathanial replied, a little wryly. "But I did defend our family, Mother. I will not pretend that is not true."

"And I am proud of you for that." Lady Ashbourne lifted her gaze to his. "Do not think that I am upset over what you did, Ashbourne. I am only glad that you did not do as the gossip mongers are saying – and I will tell my friends and acquaintances that! I will speak in such a way as to state that those who *listen* to gossip are the very worst of characters and those who defend their family ought not to be treated so."

Nathanial smiled, his heart softened by his mother's determination. "Thank you, Mother. I am sure that will not be necessary."

"It is quite necessary!" Lady Ashbourne tossed her head. "I will *not* have lies spoken of about my son." So saying, she smiled at a group of ladies and then stepped towards them with alacrity though Nathanial caught the glances sent in his direction. With a small sigh, he turned to his brother and shrugged.

"Mother may do her best but I do not think that it will make much difference." He scowled. "I am sorry, Highcroft. It is unfortunately the case that the *ton* will look upon you a little unfavorably also, I am afraid."

"Or," his brother responded, a grin on his face, "they might think sympathetically toward me, for I am the injured party, am I not? Literally, in fact?"

Nathanial could not help but chuckle, glad that his brother could see brightness where Nathanial himself saw only darkness. "You are quite foolish, Highcroft."

"I am not. I am quite sober-minded," came the reply. "Though I must say, I first considered Lady Amelia, I must now open my heart to the *many* young ladies who will, no doubt, look upon me with kindness and sympathy because of what Lord Wilcox said."

Something like joy shot through Nathanial's heart as he looked back at his brother. "Oh?"

"I am quite serious!" Lord Highcroft chuckled. "I can promise you that there will be many young ladies approaching me now. You do not know how society works as I do given that you have not been a part of it for a particularly long time, but I can promise you that while *you* may be darkened by these whispers, *I* will be the one considered with gentle eyes and soft smiles." Spreading out his hands, he chuckled as Nathanial scowled. "And with that, I shall bid you farewell for the evening."

As Nathanial watched, his brother stepped away with a broad smile on his face, no doubt ready to pursue whatever connections he wanted. Nathanial, on the other hand, was left wondering who exactly might be willing to come and talk with him or who he himself might be able to approach. Everyone he looked at quickly turned their gaze away and some turned their heads away entirely so as to make it clear that they did not want to have him join their conversation. His heart began to pound a little more, his breath catching as he meandered slowly around the room, wondering if he was going to be left only to speak with either his mother or his brother, should William deign to speak with him.

And then his gaze caught on one smiling face and Nathanial let out a slow breath of relief.

Lady Amelia.

"Good evening, Lady Amelia." He took in the two ladies next to her. "Lady Charlotte, Lady Violet."

"Good evening, Your Grace," each murmured, dropping into a curtsy.

Lady Amelia smiled quietly. "It is good to see that you have not hidden yourself away for fear of what society might say."

"No, I would not do that. Although," he continued, a slightly rueful smile on his face, "I am a little frustrated that it is as difficult as it seems to be. This is not what I had expected despite what you told me, Lady Ameila."

She offered him a wry smile. "I did warn you, Your Grace. This is not, unfortunately, something that can be easily removed from you, I am afraid."

"And yet I do not regret speaking up for my brother."

Her eyes flared. "No, indeed not! I do not seek to criticise you in that regard, Your Grace. I think it perfectly acceptable that you did such a thing. It is only a pity that the *ton* prefer to consider rumour and slander more interesting than the truth!" She let out a small sigh and shook her head. "I do wish that it would not be so."

"You worry for me?"

She looked at him, her gaze steady. "I find that I do. Your brother may also be affected."

Nathanial chuckled, making her eyes widen in obvious surprise. "He states that he will benefit, though I am not quite certain that I believe him." Seeing the obvious confusion in her expression, Nathanial shrugged. "Highcroft believes that the *ton* will feel sympathy towards him and the young ladies might, instead, look to him with consideration rather than rejecting him, as they will me."

Lady Amelia did not smile and Nathanial's spirits quickly dropped.

"They may do," she agreed, quietly, "but though they may express sympathy, there will be caution there. After all, they must not only consider him but also the family he comes from and the reputation that comes with that."

"You are concerned that no young lady would look at him with any genuine consideration," Nathanial said slowly, seeing the worry reflected in Lady Amelia's eyes. "I can understand that, I suppose."

"Which is why," Lady Amelia continued, taking in a long breath and letting it out again, "I had a suggestion I should like to make to you as regards all of this."

Nathanial looked back at her, seeing how she bit her lip and then ducked her head and instantly, his stomach began to twist this way and that. Whatever this was, it was clearly substantial and a little nerve-racking for her to speak of.

"I – I wondered if we might begin a courtship."

The moment those words came from Lady Amelia's lips, Nathanial felt as if all the air had been sucked out of the room. It was so forceful, he took a step back, his breath hitching as Lady Amelia blushed so furiously, her face turned scarlet.

"It was only a suggestion and it is not based on anything other than the desire to be of aid to you." She closed her eyes, her lips trembling. "Forgive me, it was perhaps a foolish endeavour and – "

"Why should you give yourself up like that?"

Lady Amelia blinked rapidly and looked back at him. "Give myself up?"

"You are a young lady here for your debut," Nathanial replied, his voice a little hoarse with surprise. "You are meant to be dancing and smiling and laughing with as many new acquaintances – and as many gentlemen – as you can so that you can find a suitable match, whether in this Season or the next. Why then would you place yourself upon *my* arm?"

Lady Amelia did not pull her gaze away, as he had expected. Instead, she took in a breath, lifted her head and smiled. "Because it would be of benefit to you and to your brother," she said, simply. "I am a lady of leisure for my mother and father have made it clear that I do not have any requirement to marry this Season. In fact, they would prefer it if I was to wait until next Season, truth be told, because that, they think, will give me greater clarity on the sort of gentleman I might wish to marry. Therefore, if I was to begin a courtship with you, it would assist you in regaining your standing in society and in addition, would bring nothing of significance to bear upon me. The courtship could come to an end quite amicably, society would look upon you a little better – for the daughter of a Marquess would not court 'the Beastly Duke' if he were truly so beastly – and we could also state quite clearly that Lord Wilcox's words are entirely untrue. My sister and Lady Violet would do the same, as would my parents, I am sure. Therefore, it would be a perfectly amiable solution, I think. But it would only be if you were willing."

For what was the first time in his life, Nathanial was struck dumb. He had no thought as to what to say for this generosity, this kindness towards him was so great, so significant that he was utterly overwhelmed by it. Lady Amelia was offering him this kindness simply because she was concerned for his family name, for what his brother might endure and what he himself could suffer with – and that was more than he could take in.

But what about my brother's interest in Lady Amelia?

"I accept."

The words left him before he had a chance to truly consider what it was he was going to say. The realization that, should he begin a courtship with Lady Ameila, his brother would not be able to pursue any thought of her was seemingly enough for him to agree, though Nathanial refused to let himself consider what his heart felt in regard to that.

"You do?" Lady Amelia's eyes rounded. "So quickly?"

"Very quickly indeed, though I must say I am without the right words to tell you of my gratitude at your generosity." Putting one hand to his heart, Nathanial inclined his head. "You are quite incredible, Lady Amelia. Your heart holds such a kindness, such a willingness that I can barely think of how to respond. I will, of course, treat you with every consideration and I will speak with your father first, before this courtship commences. And, when the time comes for it to end, I will be the one to take the blame. You will and you must remain entirely spotless."

Lady Amelia smiled though Nathanial saw how her lips trembled just a little. Could it be that she was uncertain about this decision?

"You do not need to do this," he said slowly, his eyes searching her face. "If you do not think that – "

"No, I very much want to move forward with this, Your Grace." Lady Amelia closed her eyes tightly, a flush creeping up into her face as though she had not meant to speak with as much fervency as she had done. "If you wish, I will speak to my father first so it does not come as such of a surprise."

Nathanial found himself chuckling. "Your father would be surprised that I might wish to court you?"

"Given that you have not come to take tea or often been in my company nor even danced with me very often, it may," came the reply, though Nathanial knew at once what he would like to do.

"Let me remedy that at once," he stated, reaching out one hand. "Might I have your dance card, Lady Amelia?"

Her eyes rounded, then she laughed and slipped her card from her wrist before handing it to him. "You may, Your Grace."

Boldly, Nathanial wrote his name down for not one but two dances, the second being the waltz. Handing the card back to her, he heard her catch of breath as she took in what he had done, though the smile which followed thereafter made his own heart soften.

"I look forward to stepping out with you, Your Grace."

"Even though I am a beastly Duke?" he asked, his eyes twinkling. "Even though the *ton* might whisper about it?"

She smiled back at him gently, nodding. "Yes, Your Grace. Even with all of that, I will be glad to dance with you for both the cotillion and the waltz."

Chapter Seventeen

Amelia took in a deep breath, lifted her hand and rapped lightly on her father's study door. Thus far, her father had taken rather a small interest in her debut Season, though he had done everything she had expected him to do and everything a father *ought* to do. What he had not done, however, was ask her details about the gentlemen who called on her, whether or not she had any particular interest in any of them or if she had danced more than one dance of an evening with one particular gentleman. Those sorts of questions were left exclusively for her mother and sister and, no doubt, Lord Stanton would expect to be informed by his own good wife should there be any gentlemen calling upon Amelia with an increasing frequency. This, however, was the reason that Amelia herself felt such nervousness. This would be entirely unexpected for her father for he would not have heard about any such thing from her mother thus far. The Duke of Ashbourne had never once called up on, had never come to take tea with her nor asked to accompany her in the park or the like. Instead, he had been rather a distant connection, for she felt as though her family knew Lady Ashbourne and Lord Highcroft a good deal better, since they were more inclined towards conversation and the like.

"Come in."

Amelia pushed the door open and, pasting a smile to her face, nodded to her father. "Father? Might I speak with you for a few minutes?"

Lord Stanton immediately rose to his feet but rather than smiling, nothing but a look of concern rippled across his expression. "What is wrong?"

"Wrong?"

Her father came around from his desk at once, his hands held out to her. "Yes, my dear. You have never come to speak to me in such a way before now. Has something happened?"

Wanting to put her father at ease, Amelia smiled and squeezed his hands tightly. "No, indeed not, Father. Everything is quite all right and I am very contented, I assure you." She watched as her father's expression changed to one of relief. "In fact, it is because I am so contented that I wish to speak with you."

"Oh?" Leading her across the room, her father gestured for her to sit in a comfortable chair while he took the one opposite. "What is it?"

"It is the Duke of Ashbourne." Choosing to get directly to the matter at hand, Amelia spoke briskly. "Father, there have been rumours spread about him through society by one Lord Wilcox and simply because of the Duke's own inclination to his own company and to book reading. He does have something of a dull demeanour, certainly but I have seen that improve of late. It is only disappointing that, when things were going so well, Lord Wilcox decided to speak ill of him instead."

Lord Stanton frowned. "Yes, I have heard what has been said, though I do not believe that the Duke of Ashbourne could have been as violent as Lord Wilcox states. I do not know him well but what I *do* know proves to me that he is not a man inclined towards fits of rage."

"He came to the defence of his brother after Lord Wilcox called Lord Highcroft a cripple," Amelia told him, seeing the shock ripple across her father's face. "I was truly horrified, given that I was present at the time Lord Wilcox said such things. I have a great deal of sympathy for the Duke of Ashbourne and... and it is because of this that I now seek your permission to accept his offer of courtship, when it is made." She swallowed hard, seeing her father's eyes widen. "He will come to speak to you of this before he speaks to me, of course, but I know that it is soon to come."

For a long moment, nothing but silence flooded the room. Amelia did not know where to look or what to say, her stomach tightening as she glimpsed the surprise reflected in her father's eyes.

"You... you expect the Duke of Ashbourne to ask to court you, Amelia?" Her father leaned forward in his chair and looked at her steadily, a seriousness on his expression now rather than any obvious hint of delight. "You are aware of the sort of man he is, are you not? He is not in the least bit delighted with company – though he has improved a little in that regard this Season, certainly – but he is also not the same character as you. You are delightful and joyous and glad about a good many things whereas he is not at all joyous and happy as regards his present circumstances. He does not seem to be glad about anything at all. Indeed, I do not think that I have ever seen him smile! Yes, he may be a Duke, my dear, but that does not mean that he is a suitable match for you. I would not ask you to accept him simply because of his title."

Amelia smiled gently, appreciating her father's concern. "You are very good, Father. I am sure that many a gentleman would have forced their daughters to accept the suit of a gentleman such as the Duke of Ashbourne without any hesitation regardless as to what they themselves felt or had because of any real concern over the man's character. You are not so. You are considerate and generous in that regard and I am truly grateful for that, Father."

Lord Stanton nodded slowly, his eyes still searching hers. "You speak kindly of me, my dear, but that does not take away what I have said. I do not want you to accept the Duke of Ashbourne's offer simply because it is he who offers it. A man's title is one thing but it is his character which is of the greatest importance. That is why I was concerned for your sister that she would *only* accept Lord Stirling once she had met him and was contented with him."

"And you show me the same kindness." Amelia put one hand to her heart. "But I should like to accept the Duke of Ashbourne's courtship." She watched as her father considered this. There was every possibility that he would refuse her, that even though she wished to accept, he might think it best if she refused. At the same time, there was also the awareness within her that she was not telling her father the entirety of the truth and that did pain her somewhat.

"Amelia." Her father sighed and shook his head. "If you wish to accept the courtship of the Duke of Ashbourne, I would be a fool to prevent it. However, do be aware that I do not think he is the right character for you. I would not like to see you upset or displeased and should the courtship come to an end, I will *not*, I assure you, be at all upset or angry. Rather, I will understand it."

Amelia's heart leapt and she could not prevent herself from smiling. "Thank you, Father. That is very gracious of you and I do appreciate your kindness in that regard."

113

He returned her smile. "That is quite all right. You are my daughter and I care for you a great deal. I only want you to be happy."

"I will be," Amelia replied, softly. "Thank you, Father." She rose to her feet the same time as her father did so, his eyes still searching her face. Hoping to reassure him, she gave him a warm smile and her father, after a moment, returned it.

"You say the Duke himself will come to speak with me?"

Amelia nodded. "Yes, Father. I wanted to speak with you first, of course, since I knew it would be something of a surprise."

Lord Stanton chuckled. "It certainly has been," he agreed, as Amelia made her way to the door. "But I shall look forward to his visit. Thank you, Amelia."

Opening the door, she smiled back at him. "Thank *you*, Father."

***

"Are you being entirely serious?"

Amelia laughed as her mother's eyes rounded, her face having gone a little pale as she looked at Amelia steadily. "Yes, Mama, I am quite serious. The Duke of Ashbourne seeks to court me."

"And... and you think to accept him?"

Again, Amelia nodded. "I can see no reason not to."

"Aside from the fact that he has all these rumours swirling around about him?" her mother protested, her eyes now wide. "Amelia, do you not understand that the *ton* will speak of you also? What will they say about you?"

"I do not care about that," Amelia replied, softly. "Mother, I quite understand that you are concerned about me in that regard but rumours pass, do they not? And I do not believe what the *ton* are saying, especially because I was present when Lord Wilcox spoke so harshly to Lord Highcroft."

This did not seem to affect her mother in the least, for Lady Stanton immediately began to shake her head. "What it is that Lord Wilcox said, does not matter. What matters is that the *ton* will speak of you in connection to the Duke of Ashbourne!"

"Mayhap they will speak well of me. Mayhap my connection to the Duke will force them to reconsider what has been said of him."

Again, Lady Stanton shook her head. "I do not think that will be so, my dear. I am concerned that all it will do will force you into the same shadow that currently lingers over him!"

Amelia's shoulders dropped. She had thought that her mother would be more easily convinced than her father but it seemed now that she had been mistaken. Lady Stanton was much more resistant than Amelia had expected.

"I do not say this to hurt you," her mother continued, quickly, perhaps seeing the look on Amelia's face, "but more because I am concerned for you, that is all."

"I understand that, Mama, but I am sure that this is the right thing for me," Amelia replied, softly. "The Duke of Ashbourne is not as dark and despondent as you might think him.

"Yes, he is! I have heard of what happened with Lord Wilcox and though I am sure it is not *precisely* as it has been said, there will have been some measure of truth to it. The Duke of Ashbourne is dark in nature and – "

"He is not!" Amelia found herself standing tall, her hands by her sides but clenched into fists as she fixed her gaze to her mother, her breath coming quickly. "He is *not* dark and despondent," she repeated, a little more firmly this time. "Forgive me for being so firm, Mama, but I will not have you say such things about the Duke of Ashbourne. I know him better than most and though he is not merry, though he is not as amiable as other gentlemen might be, there is still a joy to his heart and to his spirit which I find more than acceptable."

Lady Stanton's eyes went wide, her mouth a little ajar and when Amelia realized just how loudly she had been speaking, she immediately murmured an apology and then sank back down into her chair.

"I – I did not think for even a moment that you felt so strongly about the gentleman, Amelia."

Amelia looked back at her mother and then closed her eyes tightly. "It is not that I feel strongly about him, Mama. It is that I do not agree with your description of him for I know his character to be a good deal better than you have described."

Lady Stanton blinked and then, with a sigh, shook her head. "It sounds to me as though you are rather taken with him, my dear. I suppose, then, I can have nothing to say by way of protest, not if you have already set your mind upon him.

Amelia did not know what to say. Either she could protest again that she did not truly feel anything for the Duke of Ashbourne but given her mother's look and the words she had spoken, Amelia did not think that it would do much good.

"Your father has already consented, I suppose?"

Amelia nodded. "He has."

Lady Stanton let out a slow breath and closed her eyes. "Then, despite my concerns, I suppose that this is the right thing for you, my dear. So if the Duke of Ashbourne wishes to court you *and* you wish to accept him, then I will say no more about it."

"It cannot do any harm, surely?" Amelia put out her hands wide, seeing her mother sigh. "Charlotte is already engaged and Lord Stirling is to arrive tomorrow, all being well, and therefore even *if* the *ton* speak of me and my connection to the Duke of Ashbourne, it will not have any bearing on Charlotte's standing."

"That is true."

"And father does not see any real concern in the Duke's name being connected to ours," Amelia continued, as her mother sighed again. "I do not want to accept him if it would upset you, Mama. You know that I value your opinions a great deal."

With another sigh, Lady Stanton closed her eyes. "It is only because I have every desire to see you happy. I worry that you might find yourself broken hearted if the Duke's dark demeanour proves to be a little more sinister than you first thought."

Amelia, understanding her mother's concern, smiled gently, her heart squeezing with sympathy. "Mama, what if I find that the Duke is not as dark as everyone thinks? What if, in our growing connection, I discover him to be lighter in spirits, happier in countenance and a good deal more contented than anything I had ever expected?"

In asking this, she watched her mother carefully and saw as the small smile began to spread across Lady Stanton's face. Mayhap her mother had never truly considered the opposite of what she feared.

"I suppose, if that were so, then I would be very glad indeed, Amelia." Lady Stanton rose and came to sit by Amelia, looking into her eyes and into her face as she took her hand. "I want what is the very best for you and while the Duke of Ashbourne might be the very best in terms of his title and his fortune, I am not certain he is the best for you by way of character. You have the very kindest of hearts, Amelia. I fear what will happen should you give it away to someone who is unworthy."

Amelia squeezed her mother's hand. "I do not think the Duke is unworthy," she promised, seeing her mother smile again. "Rather, I think that I will find him to be the most excellent of gentlemen and someone who, mayhap, might be able to make me very happy indeed."

Chapter Eighteen

Nathanial cleared his throat and handed his card to the waiting butler. The butler took it and excused himself, leaving Nathanial to stand alone in the Marquess of Stanton's townhouse. Having had a brief word with Lady Amelia the previous evening where she had told him that all was well and he might now approach her father, he had seen no time to delay and had come to call just as soon as he was able.

"Right this way, Your Grace."

The butler had returned and was now leading Nathanial forward down the hallway and Nathanial followed quickly, aware of the tremor which ran through his frame. It was quite ridiculous, he knew, for there was nothing for him to be concerned about, particularly as this courtship was being undertaken solely for his own benefit – though he was very appreciative to Lady Amelia for that.

"Your Grace, I apologise that you were forced to wait. In future, I will have my butler permit you entry at once." Lord Stanton, a pleasant looking man with a warm smile, inclined his head and then gestured to the chairs by the fire place. "Please, do sit down."

"I thank you." Sitting down a little stiffly, Nathanial cleared his throat and smiled briefly. "Lady Amelia tells me that you are aware of the reason I am here?"

He nodded. "She did speak to me of your intentions. I must admit, I am a little surprised."

"Oh?"

"Not because I do not think my daughter worthy of attention from a gentleman such as yourself," Lord Stanton continued, quickly, "but merely because you have never come to take tea with her or the like. I have not seen you call, not heard that you walked in the park with her or even danced very regularly."

A flush began to creep up Nathanial's cheeks. "I am aware that my interest had been a little hidden. That being said, I would still like to court your daughter. I have been conversing with her and I find her very amiable and very warm in her demeanour."

Lord Stanton smiled with pride. "Yes, that is because she is," he replied, quietly "Amelia is kind, considerate, gentle and generous. Any gentleman in London would be honoured to have her on his arm."

Seeing the flickering challenge in his eyes and hearing it in his voice, Nathanial nodded immediately. "I quite understand, Lord Stanton. I do value your daughter immensely. I am also very well aware that my own character can be a little lacking in warmth and in kindness. I speak honestly when I say that, in being in conversation with your daughter, I have found myself eager to alter that part of myself. From what I have seen of Lady Amelia, I believe she has a great deal to teach me."

Lord Stanton rubbed at his chin. "You appear to be speaking very genuinely, Your Grace. I will tell you that I already gave Amelia my consent and therefore, I will, of course, offer the same to you."

Nathanial let out a long, slow breath. "I do speak genuinely, Lord Stanton." A little surprised that he was being truthful, he considered his words for a moment as Lord Stanton rose to get them both a brandy. Everything he had said about Lady Amelia was quite true, for he *did* consider her to be warmth, kind and amiable. In fact, he admired her a great deal. Could it be that these emotions wound their way towards something else? Something a good deal more profound? Accepting the brandy from Lord Stanton with a nod of thanks, Nathanial considered the moment he had realized that, in accepting the idea of courting Lady Amelia, he would be preventing his brother from doing so. It had come upon him with such fierceness, it had quite stolen his breath away and he had been caught with such a strength to do that very thing, he had accepted without hesitation. Why was it that he had not wanted his brother to pursue Lady Amelia? Was it not because *he* had wanted to do so himself?

And why had he wanted to do so? Was it not because his heart held a gentle affection for the lady?

"Your Grace?"

Nathanial looked up, seeing Lord Stanton's questioning look. "My apologies, Lord Stanton. I was lost in thought."

"About my daughter, no doubt," Lord Stanton chuckled, leaving Nathanial smiling. "Well, I hope this courtship is a successful one, that it leads to a happiness for you both."

Nathanial lifted his glass, surprised at how much his heart yearned for the very same thing. Even though this was meant to be for his benefit, was meant to come to an end in a few short weeks, he found himself longing that it would, in fact, lead to a happiness for them both. "Yes, Lord Stanton," he murmured, lifting the glass to his lips. "May it be as you say."

***

"Good afternoon, Lady Amelia." Nathanial bowed, having been shown into the parlor where Lady Amelia and her sister sat together. They had both quickly set aside their embroidery and had risen to their feet, bobbing a curtsy as he came a little further into the room.

"Good afternoon, Your Grace," Lady Amelia and Lady Charlotte murmured, though Lady Charlotte quickly cast a glance towards Lady Amelia that was full of meaning and not one that Nathanial was able to ignore. No doubt the sisters had spoken, though quite how much Lady Amelia would have told her sister, he did not know.

"I have just come from speaking with your father," Nathanial continued, coming to sit down near Lady Amelia, as she gestured for him to do so. "I am sure that you know already that his response was a favorable one."

Lady Amelia smiled at him and Nathanial's heart squeezed with a sudden, endearing affection for her. She was bright eyed, a gentle hint of color in her cheeks and a smile which spread light up into her eyes. She looked to be pleased that her father had accepted their courtship though Nathanial did not let himself believe that it was for any other reason save for what she herself had told him. This was a practicality, a kindness towards him which he both accepted and appreciated, but surely there could not be any sort of feeling for him? That would be more than he deserved, more than he had ever expected and certainly more than he could even imagine.

"Yes, I know that my father was to offer his acceptance," she said, as Lady Amelia smiled back at him. "I do hope you are glad with that outcome?"

"*Very* glad," Nathanial replied, with a little more fervency than he had meant. Coughing lightly, he lifted his shoulders and then let them fall. "It is what we had both hoped for, is it not?"

"It is." Lady Amelia tilted her head. "I do hope you did not doubt that, Your Grace."

"I do not."

Lady Ameila smiled. "I do hope then, Your Grace, that you will find that very soon, society will begin to look at you with greater contentment and with a kinder eye than they do at present. I am certain that these rumours will all come to an end very soon and that Lord Wilcox will not be able to do as he intends – which is to make you out to be a very unkind gentleman."

"Thanks to your help, I am certain it shall." Nathanial looked back into Lady Amelia's eyes and saw how they sparkled. His own heart leapt and with a small sigh, he reached out and, on impulse, touched her hand. "You are very kind, Lady Amelia. Please do know that I have a heart that is full of gratitude towards you for what you have done for me."

Lady Amelia smiled back at him and, much to his surprise, rubbed her thumb across the back of his hand for a moment. The brief touch made his heart quicken all the more and he could not speak for the tightness in his throat. At that very moment, however, Lady Stanton came into the room and Nathanial withdrew his hand from Lady Amelia's at once, rising to greet the lady in once. Their conversations continued long into the afternoon and, when it came time for Nathanial to make his way home, he realized that, for the first time, he had enjoyed the company and the companionship of others so much, he was disinclined to return home.

And it was all thanks to Lady Amelia.

Chapter Nineteen

"My dear Lady Amelia, I have heard the most extraordinary tale!"

Amelia smiled and then inclined her head as Lady Violet came towards her. "Good evening, Lady Violet. This is the most wonderful ball, is it not?"

Her friend waved a hand, dismissing Amelia's remarks and instead, focusing on what it was *she* wanted to talk about. "Yes, yes. However, as I have said, you must tell me at once if what I have heard is true."

Amelia smiled softly. "If it is to do with the Duke of Ashbourne – "

"Yes, the Duke of Ashbourne!" Lady Violet interrupted, grasping Amelia's hand. "I have heard that he has asked to court you!"

Charlotte nudged Amelia lightly, making her chuckle. They had already discussed whether or not Lady Violet might be one of the first to hear of Amelia's attachment to the Duke of Ashbourne and it appeared that they had been quite correct.

"Then is it true?" Lady Violet asked, her fingers squeezing Amelia's. "The Duke of Ashbourne, the one known as 'the Beastly Duke', has asked to court you?"

Amelia nodded. "It is true."

Lady Violet snatched in her breath, her hand releasing Amelia's and then pressing against her own heart. "Goodness!" Her eyes flared. "You have not accepted him, have you?"

"I – I have." Amelia's smile faded as she took in Lady Violet's rounded eyes and somewhat horrified expression. "You do not think this a bad connection, do you?"

"I do. Of course I do!" Lady Violet threw up her hands. "The Duke has a dark demeanour whereas you are nothing but brightness and joy. He does not smile whereas the only thing you can do is smile! There is a sorrow to him whereas you have no sorrow within your own heart. There is no connection there, no similarity between you."

Amelia swallowed hard, then took Lady Violet's hand again. "My dear friend, you need not think of me in that way. Yes, there are so many differences between myself and the Duke of Ashbourne but that does not mean that there cannot be any connection between us. There is a tenderness to him that is not seen by many, I think."

"Besides," Lady Charlotte put in, quickly, "Amelia is only going to be courting the Duke of Ashbourne for a short while, until the *ton* think better of him. It is not because there is anything serious between them."

Lady Violet looked first from Charlotte to Amelia and then back again before she let out a long, slow breath of relief, her shoulders dropping. "Oh, I am so very glad to hear it. You are showing him a kindness only then, yes?"

Amelia blinked, a little surprised at how quickly she wanted to refute that, how eagerly she wanted to tell Lady Violet that no, in fact, she was all the more determined to see if this courtship would lead to a happiness for them both rather than what she had agreed with the Duke. "I – I... yes, I suppose that is true. I am going to be assisting the Duke of Ashbourne in attempting to encourage society back towards him. After what Lord Wilcox has said of him, it seemed desperately unfair to me that the *ton* has begun to reject him *and* his brother simply because he is the Duke's brother! My parents have no urgency when it comes to my marriage so I might as well connect myself to the Duke of Ashbourne for this Season and, in the next Season, find myself a suitable match."

The more she spoke, the heavier Amelia's heart seemed to become. Even though Lady Violet laughed and expressed her relief that there was no true connection between the two of them, Amelia could not join in with her smiles. Now that her courtship had been agreed, now that the *ton* would soon know of her courtship, she did not seem to want to release the Duke from it. The thought of ending their courtship, of ending their growing closeness, seemed to bring an almost physical pain.

"Lady Amelia?"

She turned, only for a smile to blossom across her face, her eyes settling on the handsome face of the very man she had been thinking of. "Your Grace, good evening."

"Good evening." He held out his hand. "I must dance with you, I think."

She took the dance card from her wrist. "Because you are obliged to due to our courtship?"

He chuckled and took it from her. "I suppose that might be a part of it, Lady Amelia, but I would like to step out with you. Though, given that we are now courting, I will take your waltz! I think that should set the *ton*'s tongues wagging all the more, since we have danced the waltz once already."

She laughed, aware of the wriggling heat which wound its way up into her heart. "Thank you, Your Grace. I look forward to dancing with you again. I presume that you have spoken to some within the *ton* about our engagement?" Her gaze strayed to Lady Violet. "Lady Violet has heard of it already."

The Duke of Ashbourne chuckled and Amelia was caught by how his entire expression lit up, how his gaze was fixed to hers rather than looking to anyone else. It was as though everything within him was focused solely on her, as though she were the only one within his view and she could not bring herself to move even a little for fear that it would shift his interest.

"I have not spoken to anyone within the *ton*, though I have told my mother and my brother. That will be why the *ton* know of it now, for my mother was utterly delighted with the news." His expression softened, a tenderness in his eyes. "She thinks very well of you, Lady Amelia. As do I, of course."

"You are very kind to say so." Amelia smiled, her own heart quickening at the softness about his expression. "I am glad that your mother thinks this is a good connection. Although... ?"

"She does not know that our courtship is an arrangement, no," the Duke answered, clearly aware of her unspoken question. "I did not think it would be a good idea to upset her."

Amelia nodded, then took the dance card back from him. "Of course not. I quite understand that." Smiling, Amelia's stomach twisted as the Duke of Ashbourne looked away. She had not thought about the pain this courtship might cause Lady Ashbourne when it came to an end. Indeed, she had not thought about what her mother and father might think also. Would it cause them pain also?

"The waltz, then," the Duke said, looking back at her. "I am sure my brother will dance with you also. He was quite thrilled with

124

the news." With a smile, he inclined his head and then turned away and Amelia, her heart sore, watched him leave with troubled eyes.

***

"My lady." The Duke swept into a bow and Amelia dropped into a proper curtsy before stepping forward into his arms.

"I hear that the *ton* are rather astonished at our news," he said, as the waltz began. "Have you had a good many questions?"

"I have had a good many *looks*," Amelia laughed, though immediately smiled so that he would not think it was a bad thing. "I have been quite contented with the outcome, however. Yes, there has been surprise but that was to be expected. Especially since my own mother and father were just as surprised!"

The Duke's arm clasped a little more tightly around Amelia's waist and she caught her breath, the laughter rushing into something a little more weighty, something that made its presence all the more significant. She swallowed hard, breathing out slowly as the Duke whirled her around the floor. Did he know how she felt? Could he see into her eyes and tell just how much she desired this nearness? How much her very being seemed to burn with the yearning for more? More of him, more of his closeness, more of his presence beside her? Her eyes closed briefly, her trust entirely in his arms as he led her in the dance, her feet following his in step and in time. She had given herself up to him entirely and the closer they became, the longer they danced, the less Amelia wanted to be pulled from him.

Her stomach dipped when the music came to an end and she was again looking into the Duke of Ashbourne's eyes. When he smiled and stepped back, her toes curled with the sheer pleasure of having him smile at her.

"You dance beautifully, Lady Amelia," he murmured, dropping into a bow. "I do not think I have danced with anyone who dances as well as you."

"You are much too kind with your compliments," she replied, curtsying quickly before accepting his arm. "That is one thing you must continue to do when this courtship comes to an end."

The Duke of Ashbourne turned his head sharply, the happiness in his expression gone in a moment. "What do you mean?"

"I mean that you must continue to compliment whichever young lady you intend to be in company with," she said, trying to smile even though a heaviness pulled her lower and lower. "I am sure there will be many once our courtship comes to an end."

Amelia looked away, aware of the sharp pain in her heart as she spoke. The Duke of Ashbourne remained silent as he returned her to her waiting mother and though he smiled briefly, there was not the same light in his eyes as had been there before. Amelia swallowed tightly, aware that something within her was changing and yet, being almost afraid to consider not only what it was but what it might mean.

Chapter Twenty

Nathanial chewed on the edge of his lip as he finished writing the guest list for his upcoming ball. It was the first time he had ever thought about throwing a ball and having spoken of it previously, he had promised himself that he would do so without delay. For whatever reason, after dancing with Lady Amelia the previous evening, he had felt the urge to do so growing steadily, to the point that he did not – and could not – ignore it.

A light rap at the door had him calling for whoever it was to enter and, much to his surprise, his brother came into the room.

"Highcroft." Nathanial gestured for him to come in. "You do not have to knock, you know."

"I do *not* know." The smile on his brother's face was a little lackluster. "You have always encouraged me to give you the space you require without interruption."

Nathanial opened his mouth to protest against this, only to sigh and nod his head, admitting that his brother was quite correct. "I suppose that I have always done as you say," he said, quietly. "But that is no longer the case. I would encourage you, my dear brother, to come in to speak with me whenever you wish it. I would be glad of your company."

William nodded and came to sit down in the overstuffed chair, though Nathanial noticed that his limp was a little more pronounced. Frowning, he looked to his brother just as William noticed the way Nathanial's gaze had settled on his leg.

"Do not think that I am in any great pain," William said, going to sit down a little more stiffly. "I am quite contented. It is only because I have been waltzing and dancing last evening that I find my limp a little heavier."

Nathanial nodded but scowled. "If I had been a better brother to you, then this would never have happened."

"You are an exceptional brother," William replied, quietly. "You have cared for me, made certain that I had the very best of everything and, in that, made sure that I was well taken care of when the accident happened. I do not think I would have recovered the strength I now have, had it not been for your insistence that I get the very best doctor that money could buy!"

He smiled, his eyes holding no hint of anger. "Besides, it has not seemed to alter the opinion of any young lady."

"Oh?" Nathanial lifted one eyebrow, suddenly pulled from his morose thoughts. "What do you mean?"

"I mean that your sudden connection to Lady Amelia has made many a young lady suddenly eager for my company," his brother replied, his eyes twinkling suddenly. "You see, last evening, I spoke to not less than twenty young ladies who all came to ask me whether or not it was true that you were courting Lady Amelia."

Nathanial's heart leapt with a sudden, fierce relief as he looked into his brother's grinning face. "Is that so?"

"It is! And I managed to dance every dance last evening with a different young lady because of it."

The triumph on William's expression made Nathanial chuckle as he looked into his brother's face, glad now that what Lady Amelia had suggested seemed to be working for William, at the very least.

"I am going to take tea with Lady Emily and her mother this very afternoon," William continued, tilting his head at Nathanial. "But there was something I wanted to ask you first."

"Oh?" Nathanial lifted an eyebrow. "And what is that?"

"I wanted to ask you if you were having any particular feelings for Lady Amelia."

Nathanial's mouth dropped open.

"I know that this is not something that you or I have ever spoken of together," William continued, quickly, "but if you are courting the lady, I must wonder if you have a genuine affection for her."

Blinking quickly, Nathanial tried to think of what to say, of how to respond but nothing came to his mind. Swallowing hard, he shook his head and then rubbed one hand over his eyes. "I think very well of Lady Amelia."

"But that is all?" His brother frowned. "You have always been a gentleman who likes his own company. After all, you were called, 'the Beastly Duke' but now, I see you have altered significantly. I believe I saw you laughing and smiling with Lady Amelia last evening, which appeared to be genuine."

"It was genuine." Nathanial spoke quickly, then caught the way his brother's eyes flared. "I – I do not know what I feel. *That* is the truth." Frowning, he squeezed his eyes closed. "Why do you ask me such a thing?"

"Because," his brother said, a good deal more gently now, "had you these feelings when I first spoke of considering Lady Amelia, I do wish you had told them to me. I would have been glad to have stepped aside. Indeed, I must admit that I am a little astonished that you would not have spoken to me about this all before if your intention was to court the lady."

"I did not know – " Nathanial came up short, his feelings within him mounting so hastily, he struggled to make sense of them. "The truth is, Highcroft, this has all come upon me rather suddenly."

"Then you *do* care for her."

"Yes, I do."

Stunned at his own admission, at his own words, Nathanial blinked rapidly, seeing his brother's broad smile spreading right across his face while he himself fought shock and astonishment at what he had said. That was the truth, then. He did care for Lady Amelia, cared for her in a way that demanded he not let her go. Was that what he wanted? That even though this courtship was a sham, even though it was meant to be used simply as a way to encourage him back into society's good graces, he wanted it to continue, to grow and to build into something all the more wonderful?

He caught his breath, his stomach twisting.

"That is good." Getting out of his chair with a little difficulty, William made for the door. "I am glad to hear it, Ashbourne. After all, it is good if your heart is warm towards her when she is clearly just as inclined towards you!"

"Wait a moment." Nathanial was half out of his chair as his brother turned from the door, which was already pulled half open. "Wait, do you mean to say that you think Lady Amelia... " He could hardly bring himself to say it, could hardly let those words come from his mouth and yet, as he did so, his brother only smiled and nodded, evidently aware of all that Nathanial was trying to say.

"Yes, my dear brother. I believe that Lady Amelia cares for you just as you care for her."

"How can you know that?"

William chuckled, shaking his head lightly. "Because of the way she gazed into your eyes as you waltzed together," he said, quietly. "Because of the way she looked up at you, that gentle smile on her face as you walked together. Because of the passionate way she defended your character to those who asked about you. Oh yes, you may not have heard her speak that way but I certainly did! I was nearby when one of the ladies asked her if she was fearful in accepting your courtship and the words of defence from her mouth made my heart sing. I am surprised you have not heard those things yourself! I was sure that one of the gentlemen of your acquaintance would have spoken to you of it."

"And yet, they did not." Nathanial sat down heavily, his eyes fixed on the wall opposite though he did not really see it. The shock, the wonder, the amazement of what his brother had said was too great to take in – and yet, even as he considered it, Nathanial was entirely uncertain as to what he ought to do next.

"Well, now that we have spoken, I think it is time for me to take my leave. As I have said, I am going to take tea with Lady Emily."

This time, Nathanial was out of his seat before his brother had even finished his sentence. "And I am to go to call upon Lady Amelia."

There came surprise into his brother's face, only for William to laugh as Nathanial followed out after him, hurrying in his sudden desperation to be where Lady Amelia was.

***

"The Duke of Ashbourne, my lady."

Nathanial strode into the drawing room, his smile broad as he took in Lady Amelia, her mother and Lady Charlotte. That smile then fixed itself to his face as he looked at the other gentleman sitting beside Lady Amelia.

"Lord Wilcox." Nathanial cleared his throat, lifting his chin a little as the gentleman got to his feet and inclined his head, though there was a glint in his eye that Nathanial did not like. "I am apparently interrupting. Do excuse me."

130

"No, please do stay." Lady Amelia came over to Nathanial directly, her eyes wide with warning. "We are just now expecting Lord Stirling, my sister's betrothed. Lord Wilcox was just about to take his leave, I think."

Nathanial looked back at the other gentleman, one eyebrow lifting. "Is that so? Then I am glad I came when I did."

Lord Wilcox sniffed and clasped his hands behind his back, his lip curling. "It seems as though I am to take my leave, yes. Forgive me, I did not mean to intrude upon your visit, Your Grace. Though I have said everything that I desired to say so thus, I am glad now to step away."

Lady Stanton, who had risen to her feet when Nathanial had come into the room, sat back down again. "Good afternoon, Lord Wilcox." Her voice was thin, her words tight and there were two dots of color in her cheeks. "Please, Your Grace, do sit down. It will be a good opportunity to introduce you to Lady Charlotte's betrothed."

Lord Wilcox, seeing that he was dismissed, stepped away without another word, leaving Nathanial to look first to Lady Stanton and then to Lady Amelia, though the latter quickly and silently encouraged him to come and sit by her. Nathanial did so, wondering what it was that had taken place and why Lady Stanton appeared to be so displeased. His anger began to burn as Lord Wilcox took a very long time indeed to leave the room, speaking to each lady in turn and talking at length about how good they had all been to indulge him for so long. To Nathanial he did not speak a word, though the glance which was thrown in his direction when he spoke about being glad of being listened to was one of sheer dislike.

Nathanial curled his hands tightly into fists and kept his gaze away from Lord Wilcox, seeing the flush of color in Lady Amelia's cheeks and the spark of frustration in her eyes. Knowing that she felt the same brought him a comfort though it was not until Lord Wilcox quit the room entirely that he felt relief.

Lady Amelia let out a long breath in a whoosh, closing her eyes and then reaching across to put her hand on his. "Your Grace, pray forgive Lord Wilcox's presence and the *long* time he took to quit the room. I am sorry that you had to be in his company especially after everything he has said and done to your family name."

Nathanial managed to smile, appreciating the touch of her hand on his. "But of course." Looking away from her to Lady Stanton, he saw how she too had her eyes closed. "I do hope everything is quite all right?"

Lady Amelia sighed. "Lord Wilcox was coming to speak with me – and my mother also, it seems – about the dangers that would come from courting you, Your Grace."

Fire leapt up in Nathanial's heart and he shook his head, his jaw tightening. "I see."

"The most *impudent* man!" Lady Stanton's exclamation had Nathanial's heart leaping in surprise, though he was almost glad that the lady seemed to understand the sort of fellow that Lord Wilcox truly was. "I cannot quite believe that he had the audacity to show his face here and then speak so poorly of you, Your Grace! When Amelia has already decided to court you, he believes that he has a right to speak into that! Even though he is nothing to any of us!"

Nathanial looked to Lady Amelia, seeing the frustration flickering in her eyes, the way her mouth pulled flat. "I am quite surprised to hear of such audacity," he admitted, quietly. "Though I can assure you, Lady Stanton, whatever you have heard of me from Lord Wilcox will be touched by his own dislike. He has already told some untruths about me and has spoken cruelly to my brother both directly and indirectly."

Lady Stanton held his gaze steadily. "I do not know what Lord Wilcox intended by coming to speak to me in that way, Your Grace, but I can assure you that I have absolutely no intention of listening to a single word that gentleman said. There was only one intention behind his visit and that was to discredit you in our eyes." She lifted her chin. "I am a strong enough woman to make my own decision on such matters," she finished, then turning her gaze to Amelia. "As are my daughters."

Nathanial smiled then, relieved to know that Lady Stanton was willing to trust him and to ignore Lord Wilcox. Perhaps now he could see where Lady Amelia gained her kind heart from. "Thank you, Lady Stanton. I shall do everything in my power to prove to you that I am nothing like the gentleman Lord Wilcox claims me to be. I will defend my family if I must and defend my good name also, but I will never resort to violence simply for the sake of it. I can assure you of that."

Lady Stanton smiled at him for what was the first time since Nathanial had sat down. "Thank you, Your Grace. I do appreciate your words a great deal."

There was no time to say anything more for the door opened again and Lord Stirling was shown in, much to the delight of Lady Stanton and Lady Charlotte. Lady Amelia, however, turned to Nathanial and, coming a little closer, smiled up into his eyes.

"Thank you, Your Grace."

"Ashbourne," he told her, seeing her eyes round. "If we are to be courting then you may as well refer to me as 'Ashbourne', if you wish."

Her smile grew. "I very much wish to do so," she said, softly. "Thank you... Ashbourne."

Chapter Twenty-One

"I could not quite believe it!" Amelia shook her head as Lady Violet listened with shock rifling through her expression. "Whatever Lord Wilcox thought to do, he failed entirely."

"That is good, I suppose." Lady Violet turned her head to look over her shoulder to where Charlotte and Lord Stirling were walking arm in arm around the gardens. "And Lord Stirling's arrival appears to have been a joyous one?"

Amelia smiled softly. "Yes, it was very good. I was glad to be able to introduce the Duke of Ashbourne to him as well and Charlotte appears to be very happy."

Lady Violet lifted an eyebrow and even Amelia flushed, aware that even *she* had heard the wistfulness in her own voice. Was it that she hoped for the very same happiness Charlotte had with Lord Stirling? And that she hoped for it with the Duke of Ashbourne himself?

"I presume that your mother has shown a little more contentment with the Duke of Ashbourne, then?"

Amelia nodded, glad that her friend had chosen not to ask her about what she had heard in her voice. "Yes, she appears to be. I think Lord Wilcox's appearance brought about the precise opposite of what he had intended!"

Lady Violet laughed softly. "I am sure the Duke appreciated that." Her head tilted just a little and her eyes slanted towards Amelia. "You are beginning to think well of the Duke of Ashbourne, are you not?"

Lifting her chin a little, Amelia looked back at her friend steadily. "You know that the courtship is only to serve a purpose, do you not?"

"Yes, but that does not mean that your heart might not begin to feel something for the gentleman," her friend countered. "Is that what has been happening to your heart? I have noticed a change in you for whenever you speak of him, your expression softens and you cannot seem to help but smile."

Amelia did not know where to look, ending up dropping her gaze to her hands. "I – I am not sure."

"Well, I do not know what to advise you, given that there is still such a clear distinction between the Duke of Ashbourne and yourself in terms of his character and yours." Lady Violet sighed and shook her head. "In fact, I – "

She stopped dead and much to Amelia's surprise, her gaze went over Amelia's shoulder and to someone behind them both. Lady Violet's expression gentled, her lips curving gently as she continued to watch whoever it was.

Unable to prevent herself, Amelia turned her head and looked straight at Lord Highcroft, seeing him smile and, clearly having caught her eye, coming over to join them both.

Lady Violet flushed the very moment he greeted her.

"Good afternoon, Lord Highcroft," Amelia said, noting the change in her friend and finding herself very happy indeed. Lady Violet was a lovely friend with a kind nature and she was sure that Lord Highcroft was a gentleman of a most refined, genteel character. If this would be, then a match between them would be a most lovely thing.

"Lady Violet and I were just bemoaning the fact that we are quite without any fine company, though now you have come to join us, we cannot complain any longer, Lord Highcroft," she said, seeing the way Lady Violet's gaze jumped to Lord Highcroft's. "Tell me, are you enjoying the fashionable hour? I do not know if I enjoy it or if I find it rather difficult given the number of faces present! I can struggle to recall everyone!"

Lord Highcroft chuckled. "I quite understand. It can be very difficult indeed, I quite agree."

"I hear that things are much improved as regards your brother and the *ton*," Lady Violet said, as Lord Highcroft immediately nodded. "I am sure you are glad about that."

"Of course, though I am glad for *him* rather than for myself. My brother... " Lord Highcroft shook his head. "My brother holds a great deal of guilt over a particular matter as regards my health. It was many years ago – when we were children, in fact, and since then, he has always been grave and serious. He worries about me a great deal and that takes a happy contentment from his life. To see him smile now that he has *you*, Lady Amelia, makes not only my heart very happy but also my mother's."

Amelia swallowed hard though she did try her best to smile. While she was glad that this was true, that the Duke was happier in himself, that made her guilt rise exponentially given that their courtship was not intended to last for too long. What would happen to the Duke's demeanor once their courtship came to an end?

At the same time, Amelia began to wonder what it was which had taken place that had upset the Duke of Ashbourne so greatly, he had fallen into a darkness from which he had never quite managed to recover. She looked back at Lord Highcroft, wondering if she ought to ask him. Recalling how she had caught the Duke in the middle of the night back at his estate, a sudden understanding pierced Amelia's heart. Could it be that whatever it was he had dreamed about, whatever it was which had forced him out of his bed and down into the hallway, was the very same thing that Lord Highcroft was speaking of?

"Lady Amelia?"

She looked back at Lady Violet, realizing that her friend had been speaking to her but that she had been so lost in thought, she had not heard her. "Yes?"

"Lord Highcroft asked if we wished to take a short turn about the grounds. My mother is just there and I am sure that if I were to ask her, she would be quite contented with the idea. I – "

"Ah, and there is your brother, Lord Highcroft." Seeing the Duke of Ashbourne step out from a carriage, Amelia's heart leapt fiercely. "Perhaps we might walk the four of us?"

Lord Highcroft smiled quickly, his eyes alight. "I think that an excellent notion. Let me fetch my brother at once."

Amelia nodded and the ladies stepped to speak to their respective mothers to ask for permission to walk with the gentlemen – and both were granted it very quickly indeed. By the time they had come together again, Lord Highcroft and the Duke of Ashbourne were waiting for them. Inclining her head, Amelia accepted the Duke's arm and began to walk with him, delighting in the warm smile he sent to her.

"I am very glad to see you this afternoon, Amelia."

The informal way he spoke to her made her smile softly, her stomach cramping with a sudden, fierce heat. "As I am you. I was having an interesting conversation with your brother before your arrival too."

The Duke looked at her, his eyebrows lifting. "Were you?"

"We were. He told me... " Glancing over her shoulder, Amelia smiled to herself, seeing Lady Violet and Lord Highcroft walking together, their heads close together in deep conversation. "He told me that there is a reason behind your dark demeanour, though there has been a lessening of that of late."

The Duke cleared his throat rather gruffly, no smile on his face now. "Did he now?"

Hearing the slight wariness in his voice, Amelia nodded but then pressed her lips tight together. She wanted very much to ask him about it but given the tone of his voice, felt herself a little uncertain as to whether or not she ought to do so.

"You want to ask me about it."

"I – I do." Glancing up at him, Amelia looked away again. "Though I will not if you would prefer I said nothing. This is not something that I require to know."

There came a short silence and Amelia dared not look up at the Duke for fear of what she might see in his expression. Hearing a heavy sigh coming from him, she licked her lips and then took in a deep breath, ready to tell him that she ought not to have said a single word, only for the Duke of Ashbourne to begin to speak.

"I was a young man." There was a sense of sadness in his voice now, a weight which had not been there before. "My friends and I were playing in the gardens of my father's estate. Highcroft was present also, though I was doing my level best not to pay him much attention. After all, he was my younger brother and rather annoying to a young man such as myself." He smiled ruefully, though nothing came into his eyes. "We were playing by the pond, crossing it by a large branch which had been placed there. Highcroft wished to join in and though we mocked and teased him, he insisted." His voice cracked. "I did not see until it was too late that he had fallen in the water. When I tried to pull him out, his foot caught in the branch and I caused him more trauma. Thanks to God's goodness, he revived but his leg and his body were not without injury. I caused that."

Amelia closed her eyes, her breath hitching as she heard the pain in the Duke of Ashbourne's voice. "I did not know."

"I did not speak of it." The Duke gave her a wry smile, his free hand reaching across to press hers as it rested on his arm. "I have not spoken of it to anyone for a long time. Only my mother and my brother are aware of the darkness which clings to me still."

"But your brother does not seem to hold any anger towards you in that regard."

The Duke smiled briefly. "No, he does not. He is very good in that regard."

"Then why do you feel such darkness still? Why do you still struggle with a dark despondency?"

"Because," the Duke replied, softly, "if I had taken better care of my brother, if I had looked after him, not mocked him, not teased him or ignored him then none of that would have taken place. He would not have the limp that ails him at present. None of what happened would have taken place! In that regard, I am the only one responsible for what happened to him. And I can see the consequences of my lack of care and consideration every day."

Amelia smiled and then pressed her hand a little more on his arm. "But to linger in darkness, to linger in pain and in suffering is not what your brother wants, I am sure. Neither does your mother. So why do you insist on clinging to that?"

The Duke opened his mouth and then closed it again, his brows furrowing.

"Is that what has kept you back from everyone?" Amelia asked, when he did not respond. "You have shunned social gatherings because you are punishing yourself for what happened when you were children?"

A heavy breath escaped from the Duke and he nodded slowly. "I believe that I must be doing that, Amelia, though I have not seen it in that way before. In a way, I suppose that I believed that I did not deserve good company, that it would be better for everyone if I was not present. Now, however, I see that I did not consider for a moment that I was doing so in order to punish myself."

"You told me that your dreams torment you at times," Amelia remembered, seeing him nod. "Our encounter in the early hours of the morning back at your estate was such an occasion, yes?"

The Duke nodded, his lips curving ruefully. "Yes, that is so."

"Then I must hope that there is some happiness here," Amelia replied, softly. "That you will find a sense of contentment and even joy that will chase away the despondency within you. If your brother holds nothing against you and your mother does not either, then I can only pray that you will release yourself from the prison you have captured yourself in. I am sure, if you do that, you will find a greater happiness than you have ever experienced before."

There came no response from the Duke of Ashbourne for some moments but, when he finally did speak with her, there was a quietness to his voice which Amelia had not heard before.

"Perhaps you are right, Amelia. Perhaps I should be looking to release myself from this now." Finally, a smile spread right across his face, his expression gentling. "You are a blessing to me, I think."

Warmth rushed up into her face, her cheeks aflame. "My only desire is to be of aid to you, Ashbourne."

"You are, Lady Amelia," came the soft reply. "More than you know."

Chapter Twenty-Two

Nathanial looked out of the window and drew in a deep breath, seeing the light morning sun dappling the leaves on the trees. There was such beauty in it that it quite stole his breath away... just as Lady Amelia had done the previous afternoon.

What she had said to him and what he had found himself telling her had brought a freedom with it that he had never expected. There was a kindness, an acceptance in her eyes that he had not expected to see and that sweetness had truly touched his heart.

It felt as though, for the very first time since William had endured his accident, he had taken in a deep breath that had filled his lungs completely, as though he had lost the chains which had wrapped around his chest for so many years.

I do care for her.

Nathanial waited for the panic, for the uncertainty and the confusion to fill him but though he waited for it, though he expected it to come, it did not do so. Instead, he found himself smiling, seeming to be glad that there was now this identifiable affection within him. He did not want to let Lady Amelia go and now, even though their courtship was meant only to be temporary, Nathanial had an intention to see where it might lead.

"Brother!"

Nathanial turned his head, only to hear the door crack back against the wall as William practically flung himself headlong into the room, his eyes wide and staring. "Highcroft?" Nathanial got to his feet at once, striding across the room to grasp his brother's arm. "Whatever is the matter?"

"It – it is Lord Wilcox!" William stared back at him, his chest heaving as though he could barely believe what it was that he had to say to Nathanial. "He has placed a bet in Whites betting book."

Nathanial blinked. "In Whites betting book?" he repeated, as his brother nodded fervently. "What do you mean? What does it say?"

William swallowed hard, his eyes then fluttering closed. "It states that he will end your connection to Lady Amelia by the Season's end," he said, hoarsely. "And he is telling all of society –

140

gentlemen and ladies included – that your courtship is nothing more than a pretence. That you do not truly care for Lady Amelia and that you have done so in the hope that society will think better of you. He calls you a charlatan, a manipulator and more, telling all that Lady Amelia has been *forced* into this situation, else you were going to pull her into the darkness also!"

A red mist began to sear Nathanial's vision. "How dare he?"

"But how did he… " Nathanial rubbed at his eyes. "There has been the hope that the connection between Lady Amelia and myself would improve my standing in society – and thus far, it has seemed to do that – but there is more in my heart for her now. I do not know how he could make such statements, how he could have stumbled upon the truth of our courtship, though he does not know how I feel about the lady now, of course."

William shook his head. "I do not know, brother, but all of the *ton* are in uproar! You will not be able to set foot out of this house without someone watching you, someone whispering about you." He swallowed again. "And what is worse, Lady Amelia will be pulled into it also."

Nathanial closed his eyes, a heaviness on his heart. "And she will be spoken of poorly by the *ton* also, no doubt," he muttered, heavily. "If they believe that our courtship is false then who can say what the *ton* will think?"

His brother scowled, the fright beginning to fade from his face. "You need to consider what you will do, brother. You must do something! You cannot simply sit and wait for the *ton* to start speaking of Lady Amelia and you! You must enact a defence!"

Nathanial nodded but rubbed one hand over his chin, his heart heavy. "I do not know what I am to do. The problem is that Lord Wilcox is not entirely incorrect in what he has said. This courtship was not meant to be of a serious nature but now… now that I consider it, I see that my desire is not for anyone other Lady Amelia. I do not want to do anything to end our courtship."

"Because you have come to care for her." It was said so nonchalantly, so matter of fact, that Nathanial could not help but chuckle, despite the gravity of the situation.

"You appear to have seen it sooner than I have been aware of it," he said to his brother, as William nodded quickly. "I do not know what it is I ought to do but I certainly do *not* wish for Lady

141

Amelia to be captured by Lord Wilcox. I cannot imagine what Lord Wilcox means by stating such a thing in Whites betting book. Surely he cannot think that Lady Amelia would willingly engage herself to him?"

William shook his head. "Mayhap he believes that, in ending your courtship with Lady Amelia, she will be so distressed – or her father so displeased – that she will be contented to court and engage herself to any gentleman who approaches her, simply because it will restore her standing in society."

Nathanial snorted. "Lord Wilcox does not know Lady Amelia's character particularly well, then. There is nothing within her that would even begin to consider a gentleman such as Lord Wilcox, even if I were to end our courtship."

His brother lifted an eyebrow. "You do not intend to end it, then?"

"No." Nathanial lifted his chin, his determination growing in strength with every breath he took. "No, I intend to do precisely the opposite."

William blinked, his eyes rounding just a little. "The very opposite would be engagement, brother."

"Yes," Nathanial agreed, quietly. "Yes, I believe that it would be." With a small, wry smile, he looked to his brother again. "Let us hope that Lady Amelia will be willing to accept me... and that I get to speak to her before news of this reaches her ears."

***

"Your Grace."

Nathanial turned just as Lord Stanton stepped out from his study, coming to stand framed in the doorway, his hands clamped to his waist, his elbows akimbo. "Good afternoon, Lord Stanton." Seeing the man's somewhat dark demeanor, Nathanial let out a slow breath, a little worried that Lord Stanton had already heard of what Lord Wilcox had done. "I came to see Lady Amelia."

"Yes, I thought that might be your reason for calling." Lord Stanton still did not smile. "However, I should like to know a little more about this courtship of yours."

Nathanial's heart slammed hard against his chest. Evidently, Lord Stanton *had* heard what Lord Wilcox had said. "My brother has only just informed me about Lord Wilcox's bet," he said, coming closer to the gentleman as Lord Stanton scowled, his eyes flashing. "That is greatly distressing for me and, I am sure, to you also".

"It is, especially given that I thought this courtship was going along very well indeed," came the reply. "But now I hear that it is nothing more than a pretence!"

Stepping into the gentleman's study, Nathanial chose not to sit down but instead, clamped his hands to the back of a chair and leaned forward just a little as Lord Stanton came to stand near him. "It was not a pretence, Lord Stanton," he answered, attempting to find a way to explain what had happened between Lady Amelia and himself without telling the gentleman everything. After all, if he wanted to continue this courtship, if he wanted it to lead to something which Nathanial was certain would bring happiness, then he could not have Lord Stanton upset and determined to put distance between Nathanial and Lady Amelia. "Lady Amelia suggested that it might improve my standing in society if we were to begin a courtship. This is after Lord Wilcox had insulted my brother and, when I defended my family name, began to spread rumours about me stating that I was violent and ill-tempered."

Lord Stanton's lip curled. "I do not think well of Lord Stanton, Your Grace. That does not mean I will not listen to him, however."

"Which is understandable, though I doubt that any of Lord Wilcox's words hold any truth. They are spoken solely for his own benefit." Getting out of his chair, Nathanial began to wander around the room, gesticulating as he spoke. "I agreed to Lady Amelia's suggestion not because I wanted it for my own benefit but because I had begun to care for her."

Lord Stanton's eyebrows lifted in obvious surprise.

"I did not know it myself at the time, if such a thing is possible to say. But my brother had suggested that *he* might be interested in pursuing your daughter and given that this was the only way I could see for him to be prevented from doing that, I accepted. We have not entered this courtship for long but in truth, Lord Stanton, I can think of nothing I would like less than to end my courtship. I would be upset, broken-hearted, even, to step away from your daughter. I have come to care for her more than I had expected. I find her delightful, charming, kind and generous and I have been more open about my own self and my own life than I had ever expected to be with another living soul."

"I see." Lord Stanton tilted his head. "Then might I ask what it is you suggest to do as regards Lord Wilcox? Do you think it best just to ignore him?"

"Mayhap." Nathanial rubbed one hand over his chin. "Though I confess that I grow concerned in that regard. Lord Wilcox has made a very foolish bet and given that it was made in the early hours of this morning, I might very well presume that he was in his cups at the time. However, given that there will be numerous gentlemen who will have bet against him, I suspect he might now be in something of a panic, afraid that he will not succeed and thereafter, will be forced to pay out a great deal of coin."

A shadow passed over Lord Stanton's face. "You think that he might force the issue."

"I do."

Lord Stanton let out a slow breath, his brows furrowing together. "Then what is to be done? I could permit the courtship to continue, let Amelia make her way through society just as she has been doing but if Lord Wilcox is as determined and as worried as you think, then might he not do something so untoward, so disgraceful that her reputation could be in danger?"

Nathanial nodded quickly. "That is precisely what I would expect him to do. After all, he has never held himself back before. Think of what he said to my brother, what he spoke to him in front of Lady Amelia herself! He was not a kind, pleasant fellow to her then though he pretended to be. I have every belief that he will do whatever he must in order to win this bet."

"So he could ruin her." Lord Stanton closed his eyes. "He could force her to marry him, if it came to it."

A knot tied itself in Nathanial's stomach. "Yes, he could." The idea which came to him next was so wonderful, however, that he could not help but smile – though to Lord Stanton's obvious confusion. "Though there is one way to make certain that such a thing never happens. A way for this to be so secure, that nothing will be able to shake it."

"Tell me."

144

Nathanial spread out his hands, his heart pounding quickly as he prayed silently that Lord Stanton would agree. "I could marry your daughter."

Silence fell as Lord Stanton's eyes grew wide, though he did not say a word. Nathanial let his hands fall to his sides, waiting for the gentleman's response, only to become slowly aware of just how much he desired this. It was what he wanted, he realized. He wanted to marry Lady Amelia, wanted her to be his bride and wanted to take her back to his estate so they might make a home there together. The thought of breaking apart from her, of permitting her to one day be the wife of another was almost painful.

"Very well."

Nathanial snatched in a breath. "You agree?"

"I do. Though," Lord Stanton replied, getting to his feet, "it is not I who needs convincing. I have come to the conclusion, Your Grace, based on what you have said that you do truly care for my daughter. However, while I might consent to the marriage, it is not for me to say that yes, she will stand up in church and take her vows. That must be for Amelia to decide on her own."

Nathanial put one hand to his heart. "I would never force your daughter to marry me," he said, though Lord Stanton immediately smiled.

"I do not think that you would – nor do I think she will take much convincing," he answered, making Nathanial's eyebrows lift in surprise. "I have seen my daughter with you. I have heard her speak of you and I am quite certain that she will agree. And I am glad to know that you care for her in this way, Your Grace. I would not want either of my daughters to marry gentlemen who thought nothing of them."

Nathanial took in a breath, the significance of this moment sitting heavily upon his shoulders. "I can assure you that I think most highly of Lady Amelia. If you permit it, I would like to go to speak with her now, if she is present?"

"She is. Speak with her and then have her come to talk to me, if you would?"

Nodding, Nathanial excused himself and took his leave, finding himself directed to the gardens by one of the footmen. Swallowing hard, he went out to find Lady Amelia and silently prayed that, no matter what the outcome was, he would find a way to accept it.

Chapter Twenty-Three

"Lady Amelia?"

Amelia turned quickly, surprised to the see the Duke of Ashbourne approaching her. "Your Grace, I was not expecting – "

"Might we speak? It is urgent."

A knot caught in her throat as she saw the seriousness in his eyes, though her heart leapt when his fingers twined through hers. "Yes, of course. What is it?"

"It is Lord Wilcox." Leading her to a wooden bench, the Duke sat down as she sat next to him. "He has decided to place a bet in Whites betting book that concerns you."

Amelia blinked rapidly. "Concerns me?"

The Duke nodded. "He states that he will end our connection. He has placed a bet that he will be successful and I am afraid that he will do whatever he can to make certain it happens."

Fright began to crawl up Amelia's spine. "You mean to say that he will behave inappropriately towards me in order to garner such a thing?"

Holding her gaze steadily, the Duke's jaw tightened. "To be blunt, Amelia, I fear that Lord Wilcox might attempt to ruin you *or* force you to marry him instead, perhaps knowing that even if your reputation was torn to pieces, I would still be content to court you."

A gentle smile crossed Amelia's face at those words, realizing just how sweet natured the Duke was. It was an aspect of his character she had not seen much of as yet but with those few words, he had proven to her just how much his consideration of her had grown. "You are very good, Ashbourne."

"No, it is not that I am good. It is that I care about you." There was a fervency in the Duke's voice which had Amelia's breath hitching as his other hand sought hers. "I will not let this happen to you. I know that our courtship was only meant to be brief but I – I do not want that."

Amelia's eyes rounded but she said nothing, looking back at the Duke of Ashbourne and waiting for him to explain himself a little more.

"I think we should marry," he continued, quickly. "You must be protected and since I have come to care for you as I do, I think this is the only way for that to happen. When we are man and wife, Lord Wilcox will be able to do nothing to you."

"You... you want me to marry you?" Amelia could barely speak, her voice hoarse as the Duke nodded, his eyes searching her face, waiting for her to respond in the way that he hoped. It was clear that he had every desire for her to agree though Amelia did not quite know what to say in response.

In some ways, this was the most wonderful moment of her life and in others, she found herself upset that the Duke's desire to wed her came solely from the need to protect her rather because of any true feelings. Yes, he said he had come to care for her but that could mean so many things, Amelia could not be sure that it matched what was a growing affection for him deep within her own heart. In truth, she considered, she was actually falling in love with the Duke of Ashbourne and in that regard, she ought to be thrilled at his proposal.

And yet, her heart still ached a little. To be his wife, to marry him and take her place by his side was one thing but to love him when he did not return her feelings was quite another. Dare she say anything to him? Dare she tell him that this was what she felt?

"You have not said anything." The Duke's hands pressed hers. "This must be such a shock, I know but I do think it's for the best. You will be protected, Amelia. You will be cared for in all aspects of your life. You will be a Duchess and – "

"Yes."

The Duke's eyes widened, his eyebrows lifting as he looked back at her. Amelia's heart thudded, the silence between them growing as they looked into each other's eyes. She had given him her answer, had spoken from the depths of her heart and now the Duke of Ashbourne was looking at her as though he could not quite believe what she had said.

"You... you will marry me?"

Amelia nodded, licking her lips.

"Goodness." The Duke of Ashbourne closed his eyes. "We are to marry."

"Only if you truly wish to," Amelia said quickly, seeing his eyes open again almost immediately. "If you do not wish to, if there is any sort of regret or reluctance, then – "

"Of *course* I wish to!" The Duke shuffled himself a little closer to her as they sat together and Amelia's heart turned right over in her chest. "I want nothing more than to make you my wife."

Amelia managed to smile, aware of just how momentous a moment this was.

"And I will make sure that you are always considered, always cared for, always happy," the Duke murmured, softly. "This may be a hasty marriage but our connection will be a long one. One that I am determined to make a happy one."

"I thank you for your kind consideration," Amelia replied, though her brow furrowed over the word, 'hasty'. "Might I ask why it must be so quick? Will our engagement not be enough to push Lord Wilcox back?"

"No, I do not think it will." The Duke rubbed one hand over his chin and then sighed. "I would not have desired a Special License nor such a hasty ceremony but it must be done. The *ton* will, no doubt, speak of it at length and exclaim over it all but what else is there for us to do? If Lord Wilcox is to be defeated, then we must marry as soon as can be." His eyes searched hers. "Would tomorrow suffice?"

Amelia's breath wrapped around her chest. "Tomorrow?"

"Or the day after that?"

The suddenness of it made Amelia's heart clamor furiously but she found herself nodding, finally realizing the significance and the seriousness of what the Duke was telling her. "Very well. The day after tomorrow would suit very well, Ashbourne. It gives me time and opportunity to have one or two things prepared." No doubt, her mother would do much exclaiming and there would be nothing but frantic whirlwind of activity until then but that was what would have to be done. She swallowed tightly, trying to take it in. In two days time, she would be the Duchess of Ashbourne rather than Lady Amelia. She would not be returning to her father's estate, she would be moving herself to the Duke of Ashbourne's estate. She would be mistress of it. She would have a new life, a new situation and she would have to understand and be contented with that within two days.

"It is a little overwhelming. I can see the shock in your eyes."

Amelia nodded slowly, looking down to see where their hands joined. "But it is the right thing. My heart desires it." Lifting her eyes slowly up to his, she saw him smile. "I *will* marry you, Ashbourne. And I will do it in two days time."

***

"What do you mean, you are to marry?"

Amelia put out one hand to her sister. "I must marry the Duke of Ashbourne."

Charlotte's eyes widened. "You *must*?"

"Yes, I must. Father is explaining it to mother now. I have spoken with him also and father is quite contented with the match though he did leave the final decision in my hands."

Charlotte's eyes were so wide, Amelia could not help but laugh softly, seeing her sister's astonishment.

"It is a good thing, Charlotte. I will be glad to marry him, though I am sorry that it will be before your own."

"Oh, I care very little about that!" Charlotte waved one hand, dismissing Amelia's words. "But this is all so very hasty, I do not understand. I thought this courtship was not meant to last, that it was only to be a brief moment until society accepted that 'the beastly Duke' was not as beastly as they believed."

"Yes, but Lord Wilcox has put an end to that idea," Amelia replied, before quickly explaining what it was Lord Wilcox had done. Charlotte caught her breath, her hand flying to her mouth as worry ran right through her expression, leaving Amelia to finish her explanation quickly and quietly.

"Thus, I must marry within a few days." Her hand squeezed Charlotte's. "You will be my bridesmaid, will you not?"

Her sister blinked away tears. "Of course I will be. My goodness, Amelia, are you quite certain that this is what you want? There must be a way to prevent Lord Wilcox from achieving what he has stated – a way other than marrying the Duke!"

"There is not." Amelia spread her hands wide. "And if I am to be truthful, my dear sister, I *want* to marry the Duke of Ashbourne."

Charlotte's shoulders dropped just a little. "Then that is good." Her eyes searched Amelia's face. "You care for the gentleman, I know. But is there something more within you?"

Amelia flushed instantly, wondering if her sister had seen this in her expression. "There may be."

"You love the Duke?"

Letting out a slow breath, Amelia shook her head. "I do not know. I have not felt love before so I do not know if what I feel is love."

Charlotte smiled gently. "My dear sister, if it is a tenderness of heart, a sweetness that fills you whenever he comes into a room then yes, that is the beginning of love. That is a wonderful thing, my dear."

"Though I have not told him how I feel nor has he said anything other than he cares for me."

"But even that is marvelous!" Charlotte exclaimed. "To know that the Duke of Ashbourne cares for you is a wonderful delight!"

Amelia's lips tugged to the right. "I am not sure it is. It is certainly better than feeling nothing for me whatsoever but it is not the same as the love which is within my own heart."

Her sister lifted her shoulders and then let them fall. "That may still come. Though if I were you, I would do your level best to tell the Duke how you feel before you marry."

A twist in Amelia's stomach had her shaking her head. "I do not think I can do such a thing as that."

"Why ever not?"

"Because there is no time!" Amelia exclaimed, catching the flicker of doubt in her sister's eye. "And because I am afraid that if I do so, he will tell me that though he greatly appreciates what it is that I feel for him, he does not return such a great depth of affection."

Charlotte leaned forward and took Amelia's hand. "You will gain nothing from hiding this from him," she said, softly. "All it will give you is greater torment and I am certain you do not want such a thing as that."

"No, I do not," Amelia admitted, quietly, "But for the moment, I think I must keep my feelings to myself. There is too much to do, too much to consider and all within two short days! It must be kept as quiet as we can, however, so that Lord Wilcox does not hear of it and attempts to put an end to the marriage ceremony by objecting or some such thing."

A line pulled at Charlotte's brows. "Do you truly think he would do such a thing as that?"

"Yes, I do. Given how much he stands to lose if he does not win the bet he placed upon himself, I am afraid that he will do exactly that." A rumble of nervousness ran through her and she shuddered lightly. "As I have said, there is much still to do but it must be kept as quiet as possible. I will say the same to Abby, my maid, for she will have a great deal of preparation."

Charlotte nodded slowly and then pressed Amelia's hand. "I am very happy for you, Amelia. I am sure that this marriage will bring you a great deal of happiness."

"Thank you, Charlotte." Amelia took in a deep breath and then let it out slowly as her lips curved into a smile. "I think it shall too."

Chapter Twenty-Four

Nathanial cleared his throat. "Mother, I have something I must tell you. Highcroft, you also."

His mother looked up from where she had been embroidering. "Yes, Ashbourne?"

Seeing the look of concern in his brother's eyes, Nathanial spread out his hands. "I am to be married."

The shock reverberated around the room and Nathanial looked from his mother to his brother and then back again. No-one spoke. The silence grew heavy and Nathanial cleared his throat simply to break the quiet.

"You... you are to be married?" His mother's voice was almost a squeak and Nathanial nodded, seeing how her eyes rounded as she looked to William as though somehow, he had known of this already and had not told her though William himself only smiled, clearly glad that Nathanial had found a solution to this difficulty.

"I am, Mother. I do hope that you will be pleased for me."

"Pleased? I am thrilled!" Lady Ashbourne immediately began to laugh, her eyes bright as she got up out of her chair, her face now wreathed in smiles as she came to embrace him. "I did not think such a thing would ever happen!"

"No?" Nathanial held his mother lightly by the shoulders, tilting his head to smile at her. "Even though I have been courting Lady Amelia?"

Lady Ashbourne shrugged lightly. "I do not know what to say to that. I was glad that you were courting the lady but I must admit, I did think you both so different from one another that it would not last."

"You are right, certainly, that we are so very different." Nathanial sighed and let go of his mother's shoulders. "But she has brought such a fresh light into my life that I cannot help but flee from the heavy darkness which I have held to myself for so long."

William went to pour them both a sherry, but looked to Nathanial for a moment as he did so. "Does this mean that your concern over my limp has now finally faded?"

153

"I do not know if it has gone entirely," Nathanial admitted, "but Lady Amelia has been a great support to me. Indeed, I have told her about my difficulty, about the trial which has come to me because of my lack of action when I was a young man. I have told her of the guilt within my heart and since speaking with her of it, I find that my heart is released. I do not know what it is about her but I find that there is a happiness within myself which has been absent from me before now. I am well aware that both you, Highcroft and you, Mother, have done your utmost to help me release this guilt from myself but I have not been able to do so as yet. Lady Amelia, however, has been the answer my heart has required and now I step forward into every day with a new hope, a fresh brightness and a love which steals away my very breath."

Lady Ashbourne put one hand to her heart, her eyes shimmering gently as she blinked back her obvious, happy tears. "Oh, my dear boy. I am so delighted. You love Lady Amelia."

Nathanial opened his mouth to say that he was not certain of just how deeply he felt for Lady Amelia, only to close it again and smile instead.

"The courtship was very short, however," Lady Ashbourne continued, looking first to Nathanial and then to William. "I presume Lord Stanton has consented to the match?"

"He has. Though," Nathanial continued, slowly, "this will be by Special License however, Mother."

Lady Ashbourne's smile faded. "I beg your pardon? By Special License? Why should you think to do that sort of thing? You are a Duke! A Duke's wedding ought to be a great and illustrious occasion and – "

"It is because he must," William interrupted, as Nathanial nodded fervently, aware of just how quickly his mother's frown returned. "There has been a threat against Ashbourne and Lady Amelia."

Quickly, Nathanial explained what Lord Wilcox had done and expressed to William just how much he valued the expediency which his brother had come to tell him about such a thing. "So therefore, Mother, I must marry Lady Amelia as soon as I can. I will *not* permit Lord Wilcox to do anything to upset what we have together and I fear that, even if Lady Amelia should attend something so much as a ball or soiree, Lord Wilcox will use that opportunity to ruin her." He shook his head. "Of course, I would marry the lady still should Lord Wilcox attempt to do anything akin to that but I do not want that to happen to her. I do not want her to come to any harm. Therefore, thanks to Lord Stanton's consent, I was able to explain all of this to Lady Amelia and to my joy, she accepted my proposal. I am to go this very afternoon to seek a Special License and thereafter, we will marry. Lady Amelia is, at this very moment, preparing for the wedding itself and for the wedding breakfast which will take place thereafter."

Hearing this, Lady Ashbourne went very pale indeed and, looking at Nathanial for a long moment, slowly began to nod. "Yes, yes, I can see that this is wise. Very well, then. I will inform – "

"Again, Mother, you must not inform anyone." Nathanial smiled briefly as his mother heaved a sigh. "I would be glad to have a celebration with your friends and the like once the marriage has taken place but prior to it, no-one must know of our intention. I pray that you would understand this, Mother, for it must be taken with great seriousness."

"Lord Wilcox could hear of it, Mother," William put in, gently. "Even if you only told one or two of your friends, even if you begged them to keep it to themselves and even if they promised you that they would, there can be no guarantee that they would do. I do not think that they would do so deliberately, of course, but that it would be done without thought. A servant might overhear it and whisper it about. The gossip could spread and we could have Lord Wilcox knowing of the marriage very easily indeed."

"But what do you think he could do?" Lady Ashbourne frowned harder. "If he knows of it, then what does that matter? It is not as though he could prevent it."

"Could he not?" Nathanial said, quietly. "Is there not a part in the ceremony when the clergyman asks if anyone has anything to say which might prevent the marriage? Lord Wilcox could tell many a lie and, of course, the clergyman will be required to investigate such claims."

Lady Ashbourne's shoulders dropped. "And in the interim – which could take some time depending on what Lord Wilcox says – he could do something to ruin your engagement."

"*And* Lady Amelia," William added, grimly. "No, Mother, it is best that we keep this to ourselves just until the marriage is over and solemnified. I do hope you understand."

Nathanial watched as his mother nodded slowly, though her lips were pulled into a thin line. Aware that she had always imagined a large, grand wedding for himself and also, thereafter, for his brother, Nathanial made to say more, only for his mother to let out a loud exclamation.

"This is ridiculous!"

Nathanial looked to his brother but Lady Ashbourne was not finished.

"This Lord Wilcox, how *dare* he attempt to ruin your happiness! What foolishness is within him to write such a bet in Whites? Does he not have any sense? Does he think that he is above everyone else, that *he* can say and do whatever he likes simply to make himself happy? That seems to me to be nothing but selfishness and arrogance! This should be a happy, wonderful occasion and yet it is going to be pushed aside by Lord Wilcox's foolishness and his threats."

"Yes, Mother, it is but that is not the focus." Nathanial smiled gently and came to stand beside her, before bending down so he might take her hand in his and look up into her eyes. "What we must think of is the fact that I am to marry Lady Amelia and that I shall be joyfully happy in doing it. I promise you that, once the marriage is completed, once Lady Amelia and I have returned to our estate, I will throw a wonderful party for everyone you wish to invite so that we might celebrate this with everyone."

After a moment, Lady Ashbourne smiled and pressed one hand to Nathanial's cheek. "Very well, my son. You are quite right. That should not be what I am thinking of. I should be delighted at this news instead of thinking about Lord Wilcox and his foolishness."

"And you must promise me that you will invite Lady Violet and her family to this party."

Nathanial lifted an eyebrow to his brother as a quiet squeak left Lady Ashbourne's mouth. "I beg your pardon?"

"I am considering courting her," his brother informed them both, a light smile on his face. "I think her quite lovely and mayhap, once news about your marriage has circled through the *ton,* once everything has settled down again, I might ask if she would consider a courtship."

A broad grin split Nathanial's face as he got to his feet, striding across the room to give a hearty thump on his brother's shoulder. "An excellent thought, my dear brother. I think Lady Violet quite excellent – and she is Lady Amelia's friend also, so that can only be a good thing."

"I quite agree." Handing Nathanial a sherry, William then gave the second to his mother and after a moment, picked up his own. "Might I suggest that we make a toast to your happiness, Ashbourne? May your marriage be joyous, happy and contented and may you have all the children that you desire."

Nathanial smiled and, taking a small sip of his sherry, took in a slow, contented breath. "Yes, may it be just as you have said, brother," he murmured, as his mother nodded her agreement. "And may I have success when I go to request this Special License!"

"Oh, you will have no difficulty there," his mother promised, waving one hand flippantly. "You are a Duke and after what you have to explain about Lord Wilcox, I can promise you that it will be granted." Her eyes twinkled. "You are to be a married man in two days time, Ashbourne! And what a wonderful day that shall be."

Chapter Twenty-Five

The clergyman opened the book of Common Prayer, his expression one of solemnity while Amelia herself felt nothing more than a twisting nervousness. The Duke of Ashbourne was looking away from her, standing beside her but yet keeping his gaze trained upon the clergyman. Did he feel as anxious as she? Was he concerned that, at any moment, Lord Wilcox might rush into the church and attempt to break apart their ceremony in some way? After all, he could protest that they were not able to marry because of something he knew, something which, no doubt, he could make up but speak of with such confidence, even the clergyman himself might doubt whether the marriage could go ahead. Lord Wilcox did not like being bested, it seemed, and yet that was precisely what the Duke of Ashbourne and she were attempting to do. She could only hope that her heart, which was now solely filled with an affection for the Duke of Ashbourne himself, would not be injured for though she was sure the Duke of Ashbourne had a tenderness for her, it was not the same as loving her. And love was what filled *her* heart.

The clergyman cleared his throat, looked first to the Duke, then to Amelia's father and finally, to Amelia. He smiled gently and then began. "Dearly beloved, we are gathered together here in the sight of God, and in the face of this congregation – " There was a pause and Amelia managed to hide her smile. The congregation was only her mother, sister and Lord Stirling, as well as the Duke of Ashbourne's mother and brother – so it was not particularly large by any means!"

"*This* congregation," the clergyman continued, "to join together this Man and this Woman in holy Matrimony, which is an honorable estate, instituted of God in the time of man's innocence, signifying unto us the mystical union that is between Christ and his Church. It is not to be taken on unadvisedly, lightly, or wantonly, to satisfy men's carnal lusts and appetites but reverently, discreetly, advisedly, soberly, and in the fear of God; duly considering the causes for which Matrimony was ordained."

The clergyman continued on and Amelia closed her eyes. It was not because she wanted to focus on what it was that the clergyman was saying but more that she could focus solely on her own concerns and worries. The longer the clergyman spoke for, the more opportunity Lord Wilcox had to discover them and ruin what was to be a most joyous moment.

"First," the clergyman intoned, "marriage was ordained for the procreation of children, to be brought up in the fear and nurture of the Lord, and to the praise of his holy Name. Secondly, it was ordained for a remedy against sin and thirdly, it was ordained for the mutual society, help, and comfort that the one ought to have of the other, both in prosperity and adversity. God Almighty, into which holy estate these two persons present come now to be joined. Therefore if any man can show any just cause, why they may not lawfully be joined together, let him now speak, or else hereafter for ever hold his peace."

Amelia glanced to her right and to her left, aware that this was not the sort of marriage she had thought she would be given but, at the same time, that this was *exactly* the sort of marriage she had hoped for. Yes, it had all come about very quickly but she had no doubt that marrying the Duke of Ashbourne was the right thing for her to do. Her heart would not have been happy with any other – it was only that the Duke himself did not know of her heart. Not as yet, anyway. Would she have the courage to tell him the truth once they were wed?

"It appears that Lord Wilcox has lost his opportunity," the Duke murmured, as Amelia looked up at him. "He has not arrived, has not burst through the door and made sort of fuss. That is a relief."

"It is." Amelia nodded lightly and then turned her attention back towards the clergyman.

The man looked to them both again, clearly satisfied that he was not about to be interrupted and that the marriage could, therefore, continue. "I require and charge you both, as you will answer at the dreadful day of judgement when the secrets of all hearts shall be disclosed, that if either of you know any impediment why you may not be lawfully joined together in Matrimony, you now confess it. For be you well assured, that so many as are coupled together otherwise than God's Word doth allow are not joined together by God; neither is their Matrimony lawful."

Amelia looked back at the clergyman without hesitation, her eyes steady as she held his gaze for a few moments. The clergyman then turned his attention to the Duke of Ashbourne, studying his face for a short while as though the Duke had something he was suspicious required to be revealed. The Duke merely held his gaze steadily and, after a moment, the clergyman continued. Amelia's heart leapt as the clergyman began by asking the Duke to make the very first of his promises – there was no turning back from this moment now!

"Your Grace, will you have this woman to thy wedded wife, to live together after God's ordinance in the holy estate of Matrimony? Will you love her, comfort her, honour, and keep her in sickness and in health; and, forsaking all other, keep yourself only to her, so long as you both shall live?"

The Duke nodded without a single flicker of hesitation. "I will." Again, he did not look at Amelia as he spoke and when the clergyman looked to her, Amelia's stomach twisted sharply, her breath hitching. The clergyman gave only the smallest nod and then turned his attention to Amelia.

"Lady Amelia, will you have this man to thy wedded husband, to live together after God's ordinance in the holy estate of Matrimony? Will you obey him, and serve him, love, honour, and keep him in sickness and in health; and, forsaking all others, keep yourself only to him, so long as you both shall live?

He had barely finished speaking before Amelia answered. "I will." Again, the clergyman gave a nod and then looked to Amelia's father and, instinctively, Amelia's hand tightened on her father's arm.

"Who gives this woman to be married to this man?"

"I do." Lord Stanton smiled gently as he looked to Amelia and in that moment, tears began to burn in Amelia's eyes. Her father was delighted for her and she found her heart squeezing with the love she had for her family. Yes, she was to marry the Duke of Ashbourne but she would still love and care for her father, mother and sister – even when her sister would move to Scotland!

"Then you shall both make your vows to each other. Lord Stanton, if you may?"

Amelia blinked back her tears as her father took her hand and settled it upon the Duke of Ashbourne's. There was so much

160

happiness within her that she could barely contain it and yet, even in that, there came the concern that what she had to share with the Duke of Ashbourne would not be returned, that her love would not match his.

But it was too late to speak of that now.

"Your Grace," the clergyman murmured. "In sight of this congregation and in the eyes of God, speak your vows to Lady Amelia."

The Duke turned so he might look Amelia straight in the eye, his eyes burning with a passion which Amelia had not expected to see – and her heart lurched in her chest. "Lady Amelia, I take you as my wedded wife, to have and to hold from this day forward, for better for worse, for richer for poorer, in sickness and in health, to love and to cherish, till death us do part, according to God's holy ordinance."

At the mention of love, Amelia's tears returned fiercely but she blinked them away quickly, aware now that it was her duty to make her vow to the Duke of Ashbourne. "Nathanial, Duke of Ashbourne, I take you to be my wedded husband, to have and to hold from this day forward, for better for worse, for richer for poorer, in sickness and in health, to love, cherish, and to obey, till death us do part, according to God's holy ordinance." Her voice wobbled, her emotions rising to the fore as she looked up at the man who was now to be her husband, seeing him smile at her as she spoke. Was he truly as happy as he appeared?

"And now, the ring."

The longer the ceremony continued, the more that was said, the less Amelia began to fear that Lord Wilcox would come into the room and break apart their bond. She watched the Duke of Ashbourne take the ring and slip it gently upon her finger. Her throat tightened as his thumb ran lightly across her knuckles.

"Lady Amelia, with this ring I thee wed. With my body I thee worship, and with all my worldly goods I thee endow."

The clergyman smiled and Amelia took in a long, slow breath. Their vows were spoken, their promises made and Amelia's heart began to sing with a great sense of joy.

"Let us pray together." The clergyman lifted his hand and Amelia bowed her head, though her hand was still kept tight in the Duke of Ashbourne's gentle grip.

"Eternal God, Creator and Preserver of all mankind, Giver of all spiritual grace, the Author of everlasting life: Send thy blessing upon these thy servants, this man and this woman, whom we bless in thy Name; that, as Isaac and Rebecca lived faithfully together, so these persons may surely perform and keep the vow and covenant between them made, whereof this Ring given and received is a token and pledge, and may ever remain in perfect love and peace together, and live according to thy laws; through Jesus Christ our Lord. Amen."

"Amen," Amelia murmured, as the clergyman lifted his hand to put over their joined ones. Her breath swirled as the man took a breath and then smiled.

"Those whom God hath joined together let no man put asunder." Lifting his hand, he turned his gaze to the small group of family members, spreading his hands wide. "In as much as Nathanial, the Duke of Ashbourne and Lady Ameila have consented together in holy wedlock and have witnessed the same before God and this company, and thereto have given and pledged their troth either to other and have declared the same by giving and receiving of a Ring, and by joining of hands; I pronounce that they be Man and Wife together. In the Name of the Father, and of the Son, and of the Holy Ghost. Amen."

It was over and Amelia swallowed hard, seeing the Duke smile, hearing his breath of relief and finding her own heart filled with the very same emotion. It was at an end, it was complete and now she was wed to the Duke of Ashbourne. She was his bride, she was his wife and there was nothing now that could keep them from each other. Lord Wilcox's plans had been foiled, his debts would be many and she would have to think no more about him.

All that was left for her to consider was just how she was to tell the Duke of Ashbourne that she did not only care for him, but she also loved him desperately.

They were married now so no matter what she said, he could not remove himself from her but still, that nervousness lingered in her. When the Duke turned to walk with her to sign their marriage lines, she could barely look at him, such was her worry.

But then she had much to do. She had words to write, her name to sign and then the Duke of Ashbourne took her by the arm and led her to the front of the church. It was over. They were wed and nothing now could separate her from him.

Why then did she still feel so much turmoil?

"You are now a Duchess, my dear Amelia." The Duke walked alongside her, her arm through his as they made their way together to the end of the church. Amelia swallowed hard, seeing her mother dabbing at her eyes, her lips in a happy smile while Charlotte smiled warmly, her own Lord Stirling beside her. "Are you happy?"

Amelia looked up at him, stepping out into the sunshine and then nodding, her heart aching just a little. "I am contented, Your Grace."

"Ashbourne," he reminded her, softly. "You are to call me Ashbourne – now, more than ever! There is to be nothing between us, my dear Amelia."

The tenderness in his voice made her smile and though she wanted to say more to him, there was not time. The air around her exploded with light and laughter and joy as her parents, sister and the Duke's family came to surround them. Amelia could not help but smile, finding herself leaning into the Duke as rice and flower petals were thrown over them both.

"Have you told him yet?"

Amelia shook her head, leaving the Duke for a moment so she might embrace her sister. "I have not."

"But you must! You should have told him before you made your vows."

"There was not time." Amelia wrung her hands. "This all happened so quickly, I hoped there would be opportunity but there was not."

"Then tell him as you make your way to the wedding breakfast," Charlotte insisted. "He must know that you love him."

Amelia tried to smile and then went to embrace her mother before greeting and thanking the rest of her family. Before long, however, the Duke was leading her to the closed carriage and helping her up to sit inside it.

It was the first time Amelia had been in such a small space with the Duke of Ashbourne and though she tried to smile, though she tried to find something to say, she felt herself frozen with the awareness and the significance of what it was she wanted to say to him.

"We are married, you and I." The Duke smiled, reaching across to take her hands as he sat opposite her rather than beside her. "You are my wife. I am your husband. I find that utterly incredible, I must say."

"You – you are happy?"

Obviously hearing the slight falter in her voice, the Duke's eyes widened and his hands clutched hers, sitting forward in his seat as he looked into her eyes.

"My dear Amelia, I can think of nothing better than to be married to you. It is all that I have wanted in some time."

Amelia tilted her head, studying him. "Truly?"

"Truly. Why would you doubt it?"

Amelia took in a breath and steadied herself, her shoulders dropping a little as she licked her lips, trying to find the words to tell him what was in her heart. "My dear Duke, there is something which is on my heart which I have wanted to share with you since the beginning of this situation. I am thrilled to be your bride, truly I am, but there is more in my heart than just mere contentment." The Duke did not look away from her and Amelia, caught by the intensity in his eyes, found her breath hitching. She had begun now and there was no way for her to end the conversation without saying what it was she had begun. "There is an affection for you in my heart, Ashbourne... no, more than that. I... I love you."

The way his breath caught in a gasp had Amelia closing her eyes, her face hot as she felt the impact of her words strike not only him but her also. She did not know what to do, did not know what else to say and yet still, the Duke said nothing.

The carriage rolled suddenly, lurching to one side as the driver let out such a loud shout, Amelia's eyes flared wide, her hand clutching at the Duke's as the carriage lurched to the other side.

And then it came to a sudden stop.

Chapter Twenty Six

"Stay here." Nathanial wished with all his heart that the carriage had not come to a stop as it had done, not when Lady Amelia had told him what she had felt. There was so much he wanted to say in return, so much that he wanted to express to her but instead, he had found himself staring at her in shock and amazement – only for his driver to exclaim and pull the carriage to a stop. Releasing Amelia's hands, Nathanial pushed open the door and stepped out of the carriage, only to come face to face with Lord Wilcox.

"I have you now!" Lord Wilcox declared, triumphant. "I was told that you would be taking Lady Amelia to the church but you will be prevented, Your Grace! Do you know how many gentlemen have bet against me? Do you know how much I shall have to pay them if I fail?"

Nathanial snorted. "You should not have made such a foolish bet, Wilcox."

"I was in my cups," Lord Wilcox replied, as though this was some sort of excuse. "But I am afraid I must prevent you from taking Lady Amelia to be wed. It will not take place, else I shall be quite ruined."

For some moments, Nathanial did not know what to say to the gentleman. Did he truly think that he would be able to bring the carriage – and their marriage – to an end simply by demanding it? Yes, he recognized that he had made a foolish bet but whether or not he would be ruined by it, Nathanial did not care. Lord Wilcox was the one to blame in that regard and the consequences of his foolishness were on his own head.

"So you may tell Lady Amelia and whoever is accompanying her that there is no reason for you to make your way to the church," Lord Wilcox demanded, swaying slightly which suggested to Nathanial that the man might have already indulged in a little liquor. "If you do, I will stand before the clergyman and make my objections."

"Except there are no objections." Nathanial lifted an eyebrow. "What would you say?"

"It does not matter." Lord Wilcox waved a hand. "I will say whatever I can and whatever I wish to make certain your marriage does not take place. You will not succeed, *Your Grace.* I will be the successful one, I will see an end to your courtship and your supposed engagement and thereafter, I will keep my standing and my fortune. You tried to keep this marriage a secret but the *ton* has many a wagging tongue within it! I heard of your procurement of the Special License. I heard of your desire to wed with the greatest haste but you have now been denied that! I will do whatever I have to, whatever I must to – "

"Except we are already man and wife, Wilcox."

Nathanial could not help his grin as the broad smile which had settled on Lord Wilcox's face immediately began to fade away. The light in his eyes diminished, the triumphant lift of his shoulders dropped away completely and his expression fell flat.

"You are too late, Lord Wilcox!" he continued, his voice a little louder now as, victorious in his defeat of the gentleman, he stepped closer, leaving the lingering safety of the carriage. "I am already married! There is no-one else besides my *wife* in the carriage and we are now on our way to our wedding breakfast at my own townhouse."

"I – I do not believe you."

The thin voice of Lord Wilcox made Nathanial laugh, shaking his head. "Yes, you do. I can see your defeat in your eyes. You have lost, Lord Wilcox. I am afraid that your bet is lost and you will now owe a great many gentlemen a great deal of coin!"

Lord Wilcox took a step back, the color draining from his face. Nathanial noticed how some other carriages had come to a stop, how there was many a curious face looking out at them and he chuckled to himself, seeing the small gathering of society folk watching them. His heart swelled and he stood tall, looking them all as he spread his arms wide.

"I am wed to the most wonderful, beautiful, marvelous young woman in all of England!" he declared, hoping Amelia could hear him. "She has given me more than I could have ever asked for. She has ignored those who called me, 'the beastly Duke' and has found me out for who I truly am. Despite my failings, despite my frustrations and my darkness, she has given me her heart. She has shown me what true light is, what it is to offer up oneself out of

166

nothing more than love and generosity. There has been a change in me, both in my character and in my heart and it is solely because of her."

Turning, Nathanial held out one hand to the carriage and, as though she knew what he had intended to do, Amelia stepped out from within it at that very moment. Her eyes were rather round and she was looking here and there, color in her cheeks and her lip caught between her teeth.

"My darling Amelia." Caught up with all that he felt, Nathanial rushed over to her and caught her hands in his. "My beautiful bride. My wonderful wife. I cannot tell you how much I adore you."

Amelia looked up at him, her eyes fixed to his and suddenly, it did not matter to Nathanial that Lord Wilcox was still present or that there was a small crowd watching him. All he cared about was his wife.

"You have told me that you loved me," Nathanial murmured, looking at her, moving himself closer to her. "Do you know how much that means to me?"

She blinked. "I hoped that it would be something you delighted in, Ashbourne."

His fingers pressed hers. "And do you think that I do not?"

Amelia pressed her lips tight, her eyes searching his.

"I love you, Amelia," he whispered, ignorant now to the eyes watching them, to the sounds surrounding them both. "I love you desperately. I have not found a way to say it, have not found the right words with which to tell you this but it is true. I love you. I *love* you. And I am blessed now because you love me in return."

Her eyes filled with soft tears as she pressed one hand to his cheek. "I am the one that is blessed, Ashbourne," she whispered, as his head began to lower. "I love you."

His lips brushed against hers in what was their first kiss as husband and wife. "Not as much as I love you."

Epilogue

Having heard that Ameila was wandering through the rose garden as she often did, Nathanial hurried to find her. Seeing her walking through the rows of roses, the trellises filled with blooms of color and the air filled with wonderful scents, Nathanial paused for a moment and smiled as he watched her.

"My dear? I have something I wish to tell you." Nathanial smiled as Amelia turned to him, thinking quietly to himself just how beautiful she looked. It was a very fine summer and one full year since they had made their vows and Nathanial could not help but grow in love and tenderness for his bride with every day that passed. The welcoming smile on her face pulled him to her and he hurried towards her, his heart thrilled to once more be in her company.

"It must be urgent if you are rushing to find me." Amelia smiled and leaned into him as he wrapped one arm around her shoulders, pulling her close to him. "What is it that you want to say?"

Nathanial dropped his head and let his lips brush her temple. "First, I wish to tell you just how beautiful you look today."

She laughed softly, tipping her face up to his so that he might kiss her on the lips. He lingered, aware of the passion which built in him as he began to wrap her in his embrace.

Amelia laughed and then pulled back just a little, her eyes searching his. "You are becoming distracted, my love. Was there not something that you wanted to tell me?"

For a long moment, Nathanial could not quite remember what it was he wanted to say, only for it to come back to him. "Ah, yes. I wanted to tell you that I have had a realisation about something."

"Oh?"

"I have realised that all thoughts about my brother's limp, the nightmares which have haunted me for so long are now a thing of the past. I do not remember the last night which tormented me so."

Amelia smiled gently, her hands going around his neck. "That is because you sleep beside me, Ashbourne."

"Mayhap." Nathanial tilted his head, studying her. "I will not say that is not a part of it for certainly, it is. But it is more what you have brought into my life that has been a comfort, my dear. You have given me joy and happiness that has filled me so completely, I cannot think of anything morose. The guilt which once clung to me has disappeared completely – no doubt not only because of you but also because my dear brother is now courting Lady Violet!"

Amelia laughed, her eyes shining. "I can tell that you have not read your letters this morning."

"What do you mean?"

"I mean that I received a letter from Lady Violet where she assured me that you would have received a letter from your brother at the very same time for they were sent together. You were busy in the study this morning, else I would have come to speak with you." Obviously seeing his confusion, she smiled again. "Your brother has proposed to Lady Violet and Lady Violet, of course, has accepted him."

Nathanial's eyes flared, his breath catching as a broad smile spread right across his face. "What wonderful news!"

"Indeed." Amelia let out a small sigh of contentment. "They will be very happy, I am sure."

"Though not as happy as we," Nathanial returned, making her laugh. "But that is what I wanted to share with you, my love. I wanted to share that I have never felt this freedom, this relief before. Having you as my wife makes my heart sing in a way it has never done and I cannot help but love you all the more because of it." When he lowered his head, Amelia was waiting for him and he kissed her with all the passion and the love that he felt within himself. His arms tightened around her waist, her fingers delved into his hair and as the scent of roses swirled all around them, Nathanial felt himself to be in paradise.

"There is something that I wish to tell you, also." Amelia broke them apart though her arms lingered around his neck, keeping her close to him. "Something that I want to share with you. Something that is utterly wonderful."

Nathanial leaned back just a little, seeing the fresh light in her eyes and the touch of her smile at her lips. "What is it you wish to tell me?"

"Something wonderful," she repeated, softly. "My dear Nathanial, we are soon to be joined by a new member of our family."

It took Nathanial some moments to understand what it was that she meant. It was only when her smile lit up her features and when she settled one hand lightly against her stomach that he understood the truth. Dizziness overcame him and he gasped in both shock and wonder, a furious joy spiraling through him as Amelia smiled and laughed at the same time, tears in her eyes that spoke of her own happiness.

"We are to have a baby?" he asked, his voice hoarse. "When?"

"Soon. Early in the new year, the doctor says, though I have been told that I must make sure to stay warm over the coming winter."

Nathanial wanted to wrap her up almost at once, even though the sun was blazing with heat, such was his joy and his concern. "You must be looked after! You must take every precaution and I will do everything for you. I – "

"I am well, my dear, and this baby shall be too." Amelia's hands were around his neck again, her eyes searching his but holding his gaze with a steadiness that calmed him. "We have such a treasure here, do we not? And I know that when it comes, whether it be boy or girl, you will be the most excellent father."

Nathanial let out a slow breath, finding himself smiling as he pulled her to him – albeit a good deal more gently now. "A beautiful treasure," he murmured, gently. "One which has come from love. I love you all the more, Amelia."

She smiled and lifted her face to his. "Just as I love you, Nathanial."

THE END

Made in the USA
Coppell, TX
08 May 2024

32172683R00094